# The Curse
# of the
# Concullens

# The Curse
# of the
# Concullens

## FLORENCE STEVENSON

An NAL Book
The World Publishing Company
NEW YORK AND CLEVELAND

Published by The New American Library, Inc.
in association with The World Publishing Company

Published simultaneously in Canada
by Nelson, Foster & Scott Ltd.

First printing—1970

Copyright © 1970 by Florence Stevenson

Library of Congress catalog card number: 77-124278

Printed in the United States of America

WORLD PUBLISHING
TIMES MIRROR

*To Katharine Kidde—
and to Blanche C. Gregory—
with love and gratitude*

# Part One

MY NAME IS LUCINDA BELLEMORE AYERS—after a heroine in a novel entitled *Sundered Hearts,* which no one but Mama seems to have read. It is a great trial to me, for I should have preferred to have been called Jane and might have been so christened if I had not been the second child of my parents' union. I have a sister Jane born at a time when Mama had abandoned the fanciful for the practical. My ninth, tenth, and eleventh sisters are in order: Jane, Mary, Elizabeth. On the other hand, my eldest sister is called Oriana, my third sister is Imogen and, as I have mentiond, I am Lucinda, which people invariably shorten to Lucy. The reason that I regret the Jane is because of my surname, for while Ayers is not precisely Eyre, there is a certain satisfying similarity. Jane Eyre, you see, was always my favorite heroine and after I had read the book five times, I was absolutely determined to become a governess and practice my profession in some lonely manor house in the moors. Now my sister Jane is quite of a different mind—she abhors reading and thinks "Jane" far too undistinguished. None of us is really pleased with Mama's choices—Oriana and Imogen prefer Anna and Celia and have tried to impress their wishes upon Mama, but most of the time, she never uses our right names anyway—so many of us look absolutely alike. She had twins and triplets twice! Altogether, there are fifteen of us. Oriana, Imogen, and I are not a part of a set but Jane, Mary, and Elizabeth are, and so are Edward, Jamie, and William. The first twins—Viola and Evadne—arrived while she still had time to read novels. John and Tom are not twins, but Peter and Paul are. They were her last, when she was reduced to reading the Bible in hopes that it would augment the prayers she offered to God—more than prayers, I suspect them being in the nature of incantations against Papa's enthusiasms. Anyway, that is why I am not named Jane—even though I am both a governess and a heroine, a status I have maintained with some difficulty—for in real life, teaching is an exacting vocation. One day, long after I am gone, I am sure that women who instruct the young will be regarded with more respect than is their portion now—now when being a governess is only one way of announcing that your father did not have enough money to induce some young man to offer for you. I am sure that one day women will go into the teaching profession because of ability rather than circumstance. In fact . . . but enough of prophecy, I am afraid that my present surroundings have affected my judgment—ever since I have been here, I have been improving my gift of second sight, inherited from a Scotch great-grandmother. Where am I? Well, in the words of some poet or other, thereby hangs a tale, which I am going to tell. I simply must confide in someone and who better than those who cannot betray me since they are not aware of my real name. Lucinda Ayers is partially an alias—since I am not really a Lucinda but something like it. The Ayers is geniune.

The first link in the chain of events that brought me to my present environment was forged one morning early when Mama was even more distracted than usual because she was trying to wean Peter and Paul, who were fully two years old and had teeth as well as tempers. I was upstairs in the attic, where I usually stayed when I wanted to be alone. Though our house, a country parsonage, is large, our family is larger and overflows our eight bedrooms most uncomfortably. It was very difficult to find peace and quiet and to protect your possessions but fortunately, the attic is haunted and so none of my siblings ever ventured near it. I found it a real source of comfort and I had become used to the ghost, who generally contented herself with moaning softly in my ear or blowing the door closed pettishly when there was no wind. Those were her only ways of drawing attention to herself and certainly they were more agreeable than the incessant screaming, quarreling, and wild laughter that one heard on the lower floors. Nor did she chew up paper and launch it at me when I walked down the hall as my brothers Edward, Jamie, and Willie did, nor affect to mistake me for a mayhem-minded Red Indian from the American Western Plains as did my brothers John and Tom. Yes, on the whole I much preferred the ghost—in life, the wife of a country parson of the seventeenth century, who had been trussed and thrown into a ducking pond on the theory that she might be a witch. The water's receiving her had proved her innocence but had also drowned her. Her name is Margery.

Well, as I was saying, I was alone in my haunted attic when I heard my mother calling loudly from the third-floor landing.

"Oriana, Oriana, where is that girl?"

Since Oriana had married and left home some time ago, I realized that Mama was in one of her habitual states of confusion. I hazarded a guess that she might mean me and opening the door a crack, I called out unwillingly, "Yes, Mama. Do you want me?"

"Oh, there you are!" she snapped. "Please come down, I wish to speak to you."

"Are you sure that you mean *me,* Mama," I asked reluctantly, being in the midst of reading a new novel I had found under a pew after the previous Sunday's service.

"Certainly, I mean you, Imogen," she said.

"Lucinda, Mama," I corrected with a sigh.

"That's what I said—Lucinda. Don't be impudent, miss. Come down here this instant!" Then she screamed in a tired frightened manner, for the ghost had sent a long breath of icy air down upon her.

I abandoned my novel and started out of the attic. As I went, I heard the pages stirring and knew that Margery, ever curious, was examining my book.

"I do wish," Mama said as I joined her, "that your dear Papa had had more success in exorcizing that woman."

"Margery is harmless, Mama," I protested. I could have added that she was much more harmless than Papa, if I had wanted to remind her that she was in a delicate condition again, but I knew she would consider my observation horridly unladylike as well as betraying a knowledge no nice young girl should possess. All other indications to the contrary, Mama always insisted that she had discovered each of her children behind a cabbage leaf in the kitchen garden. Mary, Jane, and Elizabeth, who were still at an impressionable age, absolutely refused to touch cabbage.

"Well, no matter, Oriana," Mama continued. "As you know, dear Papa is far from wealthy, having so many little mouths to feed." One of Mama's failings was her constant reiteration of the obvious. I do not believe that she ever gave any one of us credit for intelligence since she rarely knew which of us she was addressing. When I think about Mama, I am visited by a prophetic dream which in this year of 1865 seems utterly unreal—yet, perhaps in future centuries, there will be some way of allowing women to enjoy the pleasures of congress without producing so many of its fruits. I realize that I am being rather indelicate but since none of my immediate circle will read this manuscript, I have decided to express myself freely. It is very difficult to keep your thoughts forever bottled in the brain for, as is the case with spirits, they ferment over the years and prove, sometimes, overintoxicating.

In answer to my mother's mention of the poverty that had left the stairs upon which we now stood covered by a treacherous moth-eaten runner, the furniture battered and soiled by generations of indigent parsons and their families, the walls stained and peeling, the curtains dingy, the windows filthy, the roof leaking, the rodents busy, all of us badly clad in clothes donated by parishioners, I said dutifully, "Yes, Mama, I know Papa is far from wealthy."

"I do not find our condition amusing, Imogen," she snapped. "Why are you smiling, pray?"

I decided that prevarication was the better part of valor. "I am not smiling, Mama, I am grimacing. I have a stomachache."

"Chamomile tea," she said automatically. "Lucy, I have found a position for you."

"A position, Mama?" I echoed.

"Yes, a Mrs. Timothy Costello, the sister of Mrs. Wyndham, has been visiting her, as you know. And she is from Ireland." Here my mother paused and sighed deeply.

"I never thought it would be incumbent upon me to send one of my helpless infants to Ireland, but since I—uh— have been walking in the cabbage patch, you understand, Imogen . . . ?" She looked at me in a manner I can only describe as pathetic.

"I am to go to Ireland, Mama?" I asked. "Why?"

"It really came about most unexpectedly. I met Mrs. Wyndham as I was coming from the draper's this morning. She greeted me most pleasantly and inquired about the family. She also praised your dear Papa's sermon of Sunday last and said he spoke so feelingly about the joys of heaven that she could hardly wait to taste of them, provided she was admitted. And——" Mama broke off, looking bewildered, "but that is not what I wanted to tell you."

"Ireland, Mama," I prompted.

"Ireland?" she said blankly. "Oh, yes. She asked me if there was any virtuous young woman whom she might recommend as a governess. Her sister, it seems, has been entrusted with the task of finding one for a family in Ireland. And I suggested you."

"To be a governess!" My dream of following in the footsteps of my favorite heroine Jane Eyre had come true! "Oh, Mama," I gasped.

She mistook my rapture, "Oriana, dear, if you only knew how it weighs upon my soul to send you forth—to cast you on the world—especially in Ireland—but there is no other way—we are so many here."

I took, as they say in the theater, my cue, "Oh, Mama," I lied. "I am loath to leave you and my family but what must be—must be." Dramatically but carefully I flung my arms around her and clasped her sideways to my bosom. She leaned against me for a second and, in lieu of tears, produced a grieving sniff. I also sniffed.

Our moment of communion having satisfied her sense of propriety, Mama became less flowery. "You'll be leaving the Monday after next."

"So soon!" I started to clap my hands, thought better of it and clasped them as imploringly as I could. "That's not quite two weeks away."

"Mrs. Costello returns home on that date," Mama explained, "and she will travel with you—naturally, you could not go alone—all the way to Ireland. As it is, you will have to part company in Dublin because O'Hagan's Keep . . ."

"O'Hagan's Keep?" I repeated. "What's that?"

"It seems that the family lives in a castle on the coast of Ireland," Mama replied.

"O'er perilous crags and plunging waves?" I asked, trying in vain to quell my excitement at the prospect.

Mama gave me a more piercing look than was her wont. "You've been reading novels, Lucy," she accused. "Upon your soul, stay away from them—they fill you with falsely romantic notions. You must learn before you are much older that life is not what novelists say it is. These authors suggest that the world is full of—of roses and instead you—you only . . ." she paused.

"You find cabbage leaves, Mama?" I inquired.

"Yes," she agreed, "cabbage leaves."

"I do not think you need worry about me, Mama," I said. "I shan't go walking through any cabbage patches and besides—aren't potatoes an Irish staple?"

She shook her head. "Such an innocent," she murmured, "quite, quite unspoiled. I hope I do right in casting you upon the world."

"Oh, you do, Mama, you certainly do," I assured her, "but please tell me more about the position."

"I do not know many particulars . . . but Mrs. Costello describes the O'Hagan family as old and aristocratic. They have a title, I believe—they are called the Earls of Concullen and they trace their descent from the Kings of Ireland."

"Earls," I said ecstatically.

"An Irish title, Lucy," Mama replied deprecatingly.

"But they do live in a castle. That's lovely!"

"Drafty, too, most likely," commented Mama. "We will have to gather some woolens together for you . . . Now I wonder where . . . ?"

"Mama," I said, "have you any notion how—many children I shall have to instruct?" I must say that I asked this question with considerable trepidation. I could only hope that all men were not so—energetic as Papa nor all women as fertile as Mama.

"Mrs. Costello was not sure as to the number of your pupils. She does not actually claim an acquaintance with the O'Hagans—but she has a friend who lives in the village near the castle and it was she they asked to initiate the inquiry. She stated only that they wanted an English governess who had a knowledge of simple arithmetic, the French, German, and Italian languages, Latin, history, English literature, oil and watercolor painting, the pianoforte and harp. I told Mrs. Wyndham that you, Imogen, could qualify in all these respects, as we had provided you with a fine education."

Confused Mama might be but in this respect she had not erred—in spite of our haphazard home life, Oriana, Imogen, and I had all had the benefit of a superior education at the dame school in the village, which during our tenure had boasted a Miss Vyvyan, a woman of high scholastic attainments, who had been a true inspiration to those pupils who had wanted to learn. I cannot remember a time when I was not eager for knowledge and, I might add, experience beyond that found in caring for younger brothers and sisters. Since I am bone lazy, it is well that I have not often been entrusted with tending the younger children. Oriana had served in that capacity before she married and Imogen still had the major part of all those chores since she was less rebellious than I and also lacked the courage to deal with the late Mistress Margery. I am sure that Mama took my dilatory habits into account when she recommended me to Mrs. Wyndham, for in spite of her problem with identification, she had a very good idea as to which one of us she really meant.

Though I found the thought of leaving home agreeable, I could not be entirely complacent about it, for there remained the problem of my wardrobe. I might run about my house in a battered cotton, inexpertly patched, might go visiting in gray poplin or twice-turned silk, but as a governess, I would need at least two gowns for the schoolroom and something that would suffice if ever my employers asked me to partake of meals with them—a proceeding I was advised I should not expect. Until that time, clothes had meant very little to me, used as I was to inheriting Oriana's castoffs and passing them on to Imogen. In our family we were taught not to dwell upon personal appearance. Papa said that vanity was a sin and that we should, as he did, keep our minds on such lofty matters as salvation. I cannot say that any of us were especially receptive to his reasoning, particularly since we, as children of a man in Holy Orders, believed our salvation assured. Yet, in this instance, one of my father's favorite axioms—*The Lord will provide*—did serve me in good stead, for by a most fortunate coincidence, the parish happened to receive a bundle of clothes donated by Lady Agatha Parrider, who lived in a manor house just outside the village. Lady Agatha was past seventy, but as Mrs. Burns, the local dressmaker, told Mrs. Tilden, the midwife, who had, not surprisingly, a fast friendship with Mama—she was young at heart and on numerous visits to London came back with highly unsuitable gowns.

"More for a fancy woman than for an elderly lady," is what I heard Mrs. Tilden tell Mama. She had not elucidated as to what she meant by "fancy woman," but when we opened the bundle, we saw that many of the gowns inside were lavishly trimmed with beads, feathers and flowers. They were mostly silks and satins, but fortunately, there was a gray wool suit that was practically new and which, Mrs. Tilden said, Lady Agatha's son's wife had had made for her, considering it more suitable for one of her years. She had not even worn it, Mrs. Tilden had exclaimed in shocked accents. Fortunately, it fitted me very well, for Lady Agatha was almost as slim as I. We were also able to utilize a scarlet walking dress and a bright orange afternoon ensemble, both of which we dyed black. Though the evening gowns were all cut exceptionally low and were therefore unsuitable for a governess, my sister Imogen, who is clever with her needle, pieced out the décolletages with lace cut from a flounce off an old petticoat and soon I had no less than five new outfits, all of which looked extremely well on me. The blacks were especially flattering to my white skin. I have not mentioned that I have a very fair complexion. I suppose that I might as well describe how I look. My mother is blond and my father has brick-red hair, and though most of the children in my family have that combination of the two colors described as carroty, mine is more the shade of dark honey. My brothers deem my eyes yellow, but I would describe them as being amber in hue, and despite all Papa preaches about vanity, etc., I must admit that I have never been displeased with my features. My nose is straight and well shaped, my mouth full and red, my eyes large and slightly tilted at the corners, my lashes long and curling. I am slender without being emaciated, full-busted but, as I have mentioned, slim-waisted and, if a sudden breeze should swirl my skirts about, interested gentlemen would see that my ankles are aristocratically delicate. In fact, as far as appearance goes, quite frankly I am beautiful and if such a confession seems immodest I can only retort that I do not believe it vain to tell the truth. Besides, I have never been conceited about my appearance—my beauty is there and I accept it. Unfortunately, I am also extremely healthy—I say "unfortunately" because I have always longed to have that interesting pallor that marks the women of Dante Gabriel Rossetti and other painters in his circle. However, I have never been able to boast that hectic flush that characterized the early stages of consumption nor have I ever been able to faint. Yet, if I am not fashionably fragile, I do have an asset not all heroines share—in common with my idol and ideal, Jane Eyre, I have developed my mind. I have read much—not restricting myself to novels alone. I have delved into philosophy, the occult, biography, biology, zoology, art and music. Too, I am considerably moved by various natural manifestations in the world about me. The sky at dawning and at sunset gives me more aesthetic pleasure than the most deftly executed painting; I am also fond of trees, flowers, lakes, rivers, and the sea. That is another reason why I welcomed the opportunity to leave my birthplace, every stone of which had become cloyingly familiar to me and which lacked another quality that fascinates me—antiquity. Our village is neither very old nor very new—the church dates back to the fifteenth century, but it is not a particularly brilliant example of its period and though it is said to have possessed some strikingly lovely stained-glass windows, Oliver Cromwell's soldiers smashed these and the replacements are merely commonplace. The oldest house in town was built in Tudor times, but its original charm has not survived generations of architecturally venturesome owners. While our house is at least two hundred years old, I cannot admire it, either. It is large and ill-planned with smoky fireplaces, a leaking roof and drafty corridors. After eighteen years of living in it, the thought of leaving it for anywhere—even Ireland— filled me with a sensation closely akin to ecstacy.

The day before I was to embark upon my journey, Mama became unexpectedly serious. I remember we were packing my trunk when she suddenly caught my wrist and said, "Imogen, try and stay close to Mrs. Costello at all times—but if you get separated in the crowds, do not speak to any strangers, no matter how pleasant and helpful they may seem. You know about the fate worse than death!?"

"Yes, Mama," I said, "I have heard about it—but I have never been entirely sure as to what befalls one. What could be worse than death?"

To my surprise, she turned a bright pink. "Well . . . you know . . . fallen women . . ." she whispered.

"Oh," I said relieved, "well—I am exceptionally sure-footed, Mama."

She sighed, "I think that your Papa had better speak to you." Taking me by the hand she led me downstairs to the library, where Papa was in the midst of composing his Sunday sermon. He looked up at us vaguely, blinking his pale eyes several times as if he had never seen us before.

"John," Mama said decisively, "Oriana is leaving us— she is going forth into the world. It is up to you to tell her about Life and—uh—what can happen to an innocent— uh—unwary young girl. I, alas, am quite unequipped to discuss such a topic." She hurried out.

Papa raised a limp hand toward his thinning red hair. "Lucy," he began—he never had Mama's trouble in identifying us, "you remember what our dear Queen said when she assumed her royal duties—she said, 'I will be good,' and she has lived by that precept ever since. You must do the same. Be good and you will not be sorry."

"Yes, Papa," I answered.

"Also remember the words of King Solomon— 'Discretion will preserve thee and understanding shall keep thee.' "

"Yes, Papa."

"Be diligent and attend to your duties."

"Yes, Papa." Impulsively, I added, "Papa, what happens to you when you suffer the fate worse than death? I mean—what is it?"

For some reason, he grew even pinker than Mama. "Unnatural girl," he thundered, "you should be ashamed of yourself, dwelling on such unseemly subjects. If you are not careful, your curiosity will be your downfall!" Furiously, he ordered me out of the room.

Later in the day, I took time out to write in my diary, "The fate worse than death has something to do with falling." It was one of my first entries—because I had only started to keep a diary when I found I was going to be a governess. I felt that it would be of value to chronicle my new life, for at that point I hoped that I would soon be having as exciting an existence as my favorite heroine.

That night, I had another unusual entry for my diary (at least I suppose it is unusual. I have never compared notes with anyone). I had gone to the attic to collect a few of my books—mainly texts on mathematics, grammar, Latin, poetry and, of course, my well-worn copy of *Jane Eyre*. I was gathering these volumes together when suddenly I heard a sound like a bucket being drawn out of a well and, for the first time, Margery materialized. She turned out to be a thin, pale little woman, whose long dark clothes were heavy with moisture. She possessed quantities of lank, yellowish-gray hair that streamed wetly over her shoulders, and she kept wringing her hands, a gesture I must confess I had never expected to witness, though I had read about it often enough. In a breathy moan, she begged me not to go to that wild heathen Papist country of Ireland and when I insisted that my mind was set on it, she warned me that I would undergo all manner of horrid experiences, each too dreadful to describe. I did not, however, believe her, for it appeared to me that her predictions were based more on her own self-interest than on any psychic perceptions she might have acquired in her astral state. Yet I did find myself strangely loath to leave her behind and it was with perfect truth that I assured her I would miss her more than anyone else in the household. My confidence was received with an icy wet embrace and a sob as she squelched dolefully back into eternity or wherever it was she dwelt.

Oddly, my confrontation with Margery had not served to dampen my enthusiasm, as it were. An hour later, when I crawled into the bed I shared with Imogen, I barely thought about her—my brain was full of excited conjecture. Though Mama had adjured me not to be romantic, I did hope that I, as Jane, would meet my true love at my place of employment. I did not even mind the fact that he would be, in all probability, Irish—I only prayed that he would not be encumbered with an insane arsonist or, indeed, any type of wife, and on that fervent wish, I fell deeply asleep.

*19*

The next morning, I was up even before dawn had stretched a tentative pink finger across the paling sky. In mounting excitement, I donned my new gray gown and fastened my older shabby black cloak. Imogen helped me pull my hair into a heavy knot at the back of my neck and pin on my bonnet and veil.

"Oh, Lucy," she breathed admiringly, "you look just like a governess!"

With solemn pleasure I thanked her and surprised both of us by kissing her on the cheek. Forced as we were to be together all the time, I and my numerous brothers and sisters did not regard each other with any particular affection and I knew that my departure was a relief rather than a sorrow for Jane especially, who would get to share my old room. At that moment, in fact, she came bouncing in, carrying a load of torn underwear over her arm preparatory to appropriating my section of the highboy. Characteristically, Imogen began to quarrel with her and I hurried from the room. Downstairs, Mama, Papa, and a few more of the family were assembled. I do not remember much of what was said, for they all talked at once and finally above their clamor, I heard the rattle of a conveyance outside and Mrs. Timothy Costello arrived to take me to the railroad station. Gratefully, I screamed a farewell to my kindred and dashed forth to meet my fate.

# Part Two

In spite of my initial enthusiasm, I did not enjoy my journey. Our second-class compartment was crowded and we nearly suffocated from the pall of cigar smoke that hung over us. Cinders flew in our eyes and we were almost deafened by the ear-splitting train whistles. Furthermore, as we chugged toward the coast, Mrs. Costello wearied me with her incessant talk about Ireland in general and Dublin in particular. She dwelt with what I can only term morbid fascination upon the terrorist activities of the I.R.B. (Irish Republican Brotherhood) or Fenian Society, which she explained, was determined to drive all English from Irish soil. As she described the hatred with which these people regarded mine, I asked her why I had been hired to instruct the O'Hagan children. I was somewhat reassured when she explained that the wealthy Irish landowners had scant sympathy for the insurgents, but still I was rather nervous—I could not help thinking wistfully that none of the problems confronting Jane had been of a political nature.

Yet, even before I had arrived at my final destination, I had forgotten much of what Mrs. Costello told me—it had been driven from my mind by the extreme discomfort of our channel crossing. In fact, when we finally left the steamer at Dublin and set foot on ground that did not pitch and toss beneath our feet and breathed air untainted by the odors of close-packed cattle and poultry, I had determined that rather than face another sea voyage, I would open my arms to Ireland and the Irish, even if the latter did hold a shillelagh behind their backs.

When we came off the ship, I remembered my mother's advice about crowds and certainly there was a large mass of people around us, all of them inviting us to take a cab or a jaunting cart—to leave our luggage with them, to buy a posy, to come to a hotel. Mrs. Costello, however, had had considerable practice in dealing with these importuners and in an incredibly short time, we found ourselves seated in a cab and traveling toward the train station, where I would embark upon the final leg of my journey.

We arrived at the station in good time and between the excitement of being so close to the start of my new life and the relief of parting from Mrs. Costello, whose inane chatter had made my head ache, I did not even regret seeing so little of the city. I bade my traveling companion an affectionate if insincere farewell, promised to write often and promptly dismissed her from my mind even before her conveyance had rumbled out of sight.

O'Hagan's Keep is located near a coastal village which, as I have already indicated, must be nameless. However, I can admit that I was most impressed by the lavish natural beauty of the land I viewed from the train. We passed several beautiful lakes or loughs, as they are called locally, and the foliage, then in the gentle embrace of early autumn, had just commenced to display its tints of red and gold. Once, I glimpsed a most picturesque glade heavy with all manner of ferns and again, I caught sight of a flashing stream hurtling down an incline. Occasionally, the woods were dense, the trees thin-trunked and pressed close together, and occasionally, there were great clearings affording you a sight of the distant hills. On one high hill I saw the crumbling remnants of a castle or fortress and below it in the valley, small houses flung about higgledy-piggledy as if dropped there carelessly from the hand of a heedless giant. It occurred to me that the light in Ireland differed from any I had ever seen in England—under its luminous glow, all colors were more vivid—some of the greens seemed actually iridescent as if lit with an inner flame. In fact, the wooded portion of the terrain was so beautiful that I was sorry when we finally emerged upon the barer roads that ran near the cliffs bordering the ocean. Yet they had their beauty, too, rising sheerly over a moiling sea.

O'Hagan's Keep is on the coast. To reach the castle, you must stop at ——— Village and hire a wagon or carriage to take you there. However, Mrs. Costello having written to her friend, I was expecting to be met by someone from the household, but when I alighted from the train, the platform was deserted. Nervously, I hurried into the station house and identifying myself, I inquired as to whether anyone would meet me. To my relief, I was quickly assured that I would be driven to the Keep by one Danny O'Toole, who would call for me as soon as he had concluded some business in the town.

I must add that I was rather surprised by the station-master's attitude—he dispensed his information accompanied by a most complicated series of gestures, eye-rollings, and twitches. In fact, when I first mentioned O'Hagan's Keep, his hand flew to his head, to his left and right shoulder and to the middle of his chest—a movement he repeated several times. Since I had grown up in a Protestant household, I did not understand his gesticulations until it was far too late for me to heed his implied warning.

I had arrived in the middle of the afternoon and Mr. O'Toole did not call for me until early evening. In the intervening hours, I strolled around the town, reveling in sights heretofore unfamiliar to me. Fortunately, it was a pleasant day and if there was a slight chill in the air, it was not penetrating. The station house was on a slight rise and as I walked away from it, I saw the village stretched before me—a place of gray, weathered houses and twisting narrow streets, upon which strutted quantities of chittering hens. Above me, schools of sea gulls wheeled and shrilled at each other, alighting surprisingly close to my feet and walking defiantly across my path. Nearer the shore, I found nets drying in the sun and small, brightly painted boats bobbing on the water. Remembering my experience of the previous night, I was inclined to avoid the sea, and at first, the little rills of ripples running crosswise over the foamy surface of the ocean filled me with queasiness. However, the larger breakers rolling in from the distance and crashing heavily on the shore had a sort of primitive beauty that compelled my admiration. After all, I had never actually stood so close to it and as

*25*

the chastened waves slid over the sands toward me and I danced back out of reach, I felt as if I were almost playing a game with them. Suddenly, the sea seemed much less terrifying and as its companion winds impudently lifted my skirts, I found myself possessed with a strong desire to plunge beneath those bubbling waves. No doubt those who read my words will be shocked when I admit that I actually wished I were not burdened by such quantities of clothes—that I could doff them all and feel both wind and water on my unprotected body. I find that I often have such unconventional desires and again I wonder if—in a future century—ah, well, why speculate—one must live in the present . . .

Eventually, I turned my back on the shoreline, adjusted my windblown attire and drew the veil I had worn throughout my journey down over my face—then I walked uphill into the village. I did not see many people about. The place seemed very quiet—almost too quiet, compared with the bustle of Dublin and even with the other towns through which the train had chugged. Yet, since sundry shops were open and smoke issued from many chimneys, I assumed that behind their closely drawn curtains, the inhabitants were probably busy at their household chores. Feeling a little weary, I started back to the railroad station and on the way, I encountered a small group of women evidently returning from a market, for they carried quantities of produce. Though I did not lift my veil, I nodded tentatively, but they merely stared at me in a hard, hostile manner and quickened their steps. Again, I noticed that peculiar gesture made by several of them. Though I was rather surprised by their unfriendly attitude, I decided to be philosophical about it. After all, different countries have different customs.

It was more difficult to be philosophical about my long wait in the station. It was nearly dusk when I saw a farmer's cart finally drive up. Guiding the reins of a spirited black pony was a lean man in battered leather breeches and a stained workshirt. As I hurried across the platform, I noticed that he was very pale with a tuft of carroty red hair standing nearly straight up on his narrow head. I could not like the sharp appraising glance he directed at me and my voice was chill as I inquired, "Are you Danny O'Toole?"

26

"I am that," he replied, "and you'll be the fine English-woman they've hired."

Though his remark was innocuous, the tone in which it was delivered was tinged with a mockery that intensified my initial dislike. In some of the novels I had read, the young master, in disguise, often came down to the village to meet the governess. I sincerely hoped that Danny O'Toole was, as he seemed to be, a mere handyman. However, I answered him politely, "I am Miss Ayers."

After another sharp glance, he observed with a grimace I hoped was a smile twisting his thin lips, "And you're off to O'Hagan's Keep?"

Finding the question superfluous, I merely nodded.

"You'll think it uncommon strange at first," he observed, "but as an Englishwoman, I suppose you're used to queer folk."

I opened, then closed my mouth on a sharp retort. As it was he who would drive me to the castle, I thought it better not to antagonize him.

He had, however, no such qualms regarding me. "Why do you wear that thick veil over your face? I suppose you'll be ugly as sin?"

Resolutely, I kept my voice carefully even and calm as I answered, "My looks or the lack of them are no concern of yours, sir. Shall we be on our way, please?"

At that, he laughed. I did not like his laughter any more than his conversation, for it was soundless, distorting rather than illuminating his pale features. "Very well, Miss High-and-Mighty, we'll be off." He slammed my trunk onto the cart with a force that made his skittish pony jump nervously. I backed away hastily, uttering an exclamation, at which he emitted another horrid soundless laugh. Don't worry about Moira, here," he said, pulling the beast's forelock, "she's used to sudden shocks."

I did not inquire into his meaning, for I was annoyed with myself for allowing him to see my discomfiture. I felt somehow that the more poised I appeared, the better I would fare with Mr. O'Toole and with my employers, too. Yet, as he handed me into the cart, I was hard put not to shudder at his touch, which was cold as a fish in the larder. As soon as I was seated, I surreptitiously rubbed my hand but I did not quite succeed in eradicating that unpleasant sensation. I was heartily pleased that the seat in front was too narrow to support the two of us, for I should have hated to be jounced against him by the motion of the cart.

It was a very rough road and to my distress, it seemed nearly untraveled. Despite our proximity to the sea, the area through which we went was deeply wooded—the trees stood so close together, I could scarcely see between them and in the deepening twilight, I heard all manner of unfamiliar noises, probably, I hoped, the strange cries of emerging nocturnal animals and birds. The thickness of my veil dimmed the remaining light even more, but I did not want to lift it for fear Mr. O'Toole might turn around. Though I was, at that time, innocent in the ways of the world, I did know that my beauty had a potent effect on the opposite sex of all ages and occupations, and despite his disparaging remarks about the English, I had no doubts but that Mr. O'Toole would be similarly affected.

We drove for such a long time that I began to despair of ever reaching our destination and, to add to my discomfort, a heavy mist swirled in from the sea, blotting out all landmarks—chilling my body and my heart as well, and though I am not superstitious nor generally awed by natural phenomena such as lightning, thunder, wind, or rain, I wondered if there were not something peculiarly sinister about this dismal vapor.

On the other hand, Mr. O'Toole was completely undaunted by it. He merely clicked his tongue at his pony, urging her on. She really needed no such admonitions, for her pace never changed—it remained remarkably steady for such a fractious animal.

I believe we traveled in the fog for about a quarter of an hour, but it seemed much longer to me—I really hated it—for I felt cut off from the world and my fellow men—caught inside a dreary gray tunnel inhabited only by myself, O'Toole, and the pony—we three together for eternity. Then, as I was beginning to think I could stand this oppressive ride no longer, we came out of the forest onto a long curving roadway where, despite the mists, I could discern the flattened, wind-stunted shapes of pine trees, growing at intervals on the other side of a low rocky wall, evidently built to protect travelers from the cliff's edge. Though I could see little, I guessed us to be high over the ocean, for far below me I could hear it pummeling the shore. Since we no longer had the forest to protect us, moisture-laden sea winds shrieked in my ear and above their incessant howling, I heard another strange sound— the horse's hooves and cartwheels struck the road with a hollow ring. However, in another few seconds I had ceased to puzzle over it, for we started to ascend a steep hill and I had all I could do to keep from sliding ignominiously off my seat.

"Keep a tight hold on yourself," counseled Mr. O'Toole, unnecessarily, as I clung desperately to the side of the cart. While I struggled to stay upright, panic warred with indignation, for had not Danny O'Toole been occupied with his errands, we might have avoided arriving at this late and chilling hour. His employers must have known their miserable climate well enough to spare me such discomfort. Though I was aware that governesses were considered of little importance, this indifference was positively inhuman!

At length that ordeal was over, too, for we attained the summit of the hill and facing us was an immense structure of weathered stone, the outlines of which I could barely distinguish. In a few more moments, we had arrived at a rough wooden gate which, in response to a piercing whistle from Mr. O'Toole, opened to admit us. We drove into a large courtyard and again the horse's hooves elicited a hollow ring from the stones beneath.

Mr. O'Toole brought Moira to a halt and another man came running to hold her while he assisted me from my perch. It seemed to me that as he lifted me down, his chill clasp lingered far too long on my waist, but I decided not to chide him—I was much too eager to get out of that dank night air. A second later, my wish was granted—in one gesture, or so it had appeared to me, O'Toole thrust me into an open doorway which in turn led to an immense hall and though the fog remained behind me in the courtyard, it was almost as dim and shadowy as the misty landscape I had just quitted. I say almost because there was a fire smoldering on a huge central hearth and by the glow from its flames I could just see tapestries and shields hung on the walls and below them at various intervals polished suits of armor. Though the fire had burned low, I longed to stand beside it and capture the remnants of its heat but timidity kept me huddled in the entrance. Thinking about Jane Eyre's cozy reception at Thornfield, I was rather expecting a pleasant little housekeeper to appear and escort me to her chintz-hung parlor where there would be tea, toast, and jam. Yet, even as I formed this wish, I heard a low laugh behind me and saw my own shadow together with another dance upon the newly il- lumined wall, as a voice with an odd foreign intonation observed:

"Ah, the English governess, I presume—but in disguise. You are Miss Ayers, are you not?"

Startled, I turned to find a tall man holding a branch of candles. If his accent had been odd, his appearance was even more unusual. His eyes were almond-shaped, his brows slanted, his skin was a golden olive, but his hair, which should have been inky black and straight, was chestnut brown and wavy.

I am afraid that my amazement was mirrored in my eyes, for a slight derisive smile twisted his full lips. "My name," he said softly, "is Dimitri . . . Dimitri O'Hagan."

"Dimitri!" I could not help exclaiming. Embarrassed, I quickly added, "I beg your pardon, *Mr.* O'Hagan."*

"Please do not," he answered, his smile widening to expose very even white teeth. "You'll be thinking Dimitri and O'Hagan an impossible combination, no doubt. My father was a younger son of this house who traveled extensively—one of the countries that he visited being the benighted land of Russia. My mother is a princess from an estate close to Outer Mongolia. You will meet her tomor- row."

"That will be an honor," I said, feeling complimented that he thought enough of me to impart this portion of his family history.

"You will meet her on one condition," he continued, "that being that you'll lift your veil and show me your face—the O'Hagans do not like buying pigs in pokes."

Though I was hardly gratified by his analogy, I could not rebuff an employer as I had Danny O'Toole. "Of course, sir," I assented graciously, "now that I no longer need its protection."

He raised his eyebrows and his smile became a grin. "Hopefully, Miss Ayers."

I could not, however, comply with his request as quick-

---

* Here, I must beg the reader's indulgence—I must refer to Dimitri O'Hagan by his given name in the text because there are so many Mr. O'Hagans in the castle that it would be confusing were I to observe the proprieties attendant on nomenclature.

ly as I chose, for I found that my veil had become entangled in the pins I had used to secure my hair. Eventually, I managed to free it, but as I pulled it off, my hair fell down on my shoulders in its usual profusion of dark gold curls. I murmured an apology but he did not heed it—he seemed, indeed, to be struck dumb, as he stared at me. His reaction was a refined reflection of the admiration I was accustomed to receive from the country bumpkins around home. His mouth did not actually fall open, but his lips did part slightly and his eyes certainly widened.

"Great God in Heaven," he exclaimed, "you are an Englishwoman!"

"On both sides," I replied icily.

"It's amazing," he gasped, "and what is even more astonishing to me—is that you decided to become a governess."

"I am sufficiently learned," I retorted, "I know French, German, Italian, mathematics . . ."

"Enough, enough, it's not to me that you must recite your qualifications. I have no children. However, my dear young lady, if you'd be taking a word of advice . . ."

I was destined not to hear a syllable of his advice, for behind me another voice observed, "Well, Dimitri, is this our English lady?"

I turned quickly to find a tall plump blond woman dressed in a heavy silk gown over which she had draped a fine paisley shawl. She had a full pretty face dominated by large blue-gray eyes with which she now surveyed me critically. My hands flew to my hair.

"Ohhh, I—I am afraid you find me sadly disheveled," I began, "I——"

Before I could continue, she laughed. "I do that," she observed in a pleasant voice just slightly tinged with the accent of the country, "and rather sooner than is generally the case."

"Kathleen, Kathleen," groaned Dimitri, "will you ruin my reputation so early in the game?" He turned to me. "This is the Countess of Concullen, Lady Kathleen O'Hagan, who is mother of Marra and Kevin and aunt of Brian—the brats you've been engaged to try and instruct."

"Only three children?" I said.

"Three which you'll find more than enough," Dimitri assured me.

Lady Kathleen raised fair brows, "Spoken like an uncle," she commented, "though Dimitri is really their cousin."

"We are all cousins, here—practically," Dimitri asserted, a strange expression in his oblique dark eyes.

I felt, indeed, as if he were trying to give me some sort of warning but decided almost immediately that my imagination, already overstimulated by my drive to the castle, my fatigue, famine, and *Jane Eyre,* was up to its usual tricks and, in another instant, as it happens, all my incipient fears were allayed by Lady Kathleen's welcome suggestion that I might enjoy a bit of supper.

Upon my immediate and enthusiastic affirmative, she and Dimitri, who still held his branch of candles, escorted me across the great hall into a passageway and thence to a smaller octagonal chamber in which another fire burned brightly. A large oil lamp descending from the center of the ceiling showed me high slitted windows, leading me to believe that we were in a tower. Even more interesting to me, however, was a sideboard laden with all manner of cold meats, preserves, pasties, and a large silver samovar under which flickered an alcohol flame. I was overwhelmed by the sight of such a lavish repast, especially since I had been expecting tea, toast, and jam.

Yet, though my hosts cordially invited me to eat, to my surprise and chagrin, I was unable to swallow more than the barest morsel. Suddenly, I was intensely tired and in the close warmth of the room, I could hardly keep my eyes open. However, having no notion of what a governess might or might not say, I dared not complain. Again, Lady Kathleen rescued me. "You're probably sadly tired, Miss Ayers. Would you like to go to your room?"

"Indeed, I should," I told her gratefully.

I was destined, however, to have quite a lengthy walk before I reached this eyrie. We went upstairs, through passages, around bends until I was nearly breathless and privately convinced that only a guidebook would enable me to reach the main hall again. Too, I was rather oppressed by the evidences that help was either scarce or careless, for great cobwebs hung in corners and little balls of dust eddied beneath my feet.

My chamber, reached at last, proved to be worth the

journey; it was very large and being in another tower, it was well supplied with windows, which had evidently been remodeled from their original slits into wide appertures, each with a comfortable cushioned seat. Between them there was a huge fireplace in which several logs were burning. Even more inviting was a richly carved bed hung with silken curtains and made up with fine linen sheets and puffy pillows. I longed to sink into it but dutifully allowed Lady Kathleen to show me an immense clothespress and then, wonder of all wonders, she opened a smaller door and displayed a bathroom complete with tub and shower!

"We had it converted from the old powder closet," she explained, "and there'll be hot water cans brought to you in the morning."

I nodded, too overcome to speak. None of the novels I have read, including *Jane Eyre,* ever devoted a sentence to sanitary facilities, preferring, I suppose, to draw a veil of sensibility over such bodily functions. However, I do feel that I should mention that the chamber Lady Kathleen had just revealed was as unusual in my own experience as it was luxurious. In our house, conditions are dreadfully inconvenient—involving an outdoor cubicle which one visits reluctantly of an icy winter morning and even more reluctantly during the summer. Washing is accomplished with bowls and pitchers, our tin bathtubs being only large enough to accommodate the younger children.

Having shown me this gem, Lady Kathleen smiled at me, "I'll leave you now, Miss Ayers, and hope you have a pleasant rest." She paused and her expression grew grave. "If you hear any unusual noises in the night, don't pay them any mind. This is an old, old building and there are many crevices through which the wind can creep."

I smiled brightly, not so much because of what she had just told me, but because I had been expecting it. Similar remarks had been addressed to nearly all the heroines in all the books I had read. I answered in kind, "Oh, I am sure I'll sleep soundly enough, Lady Kathleen." I eyed the bed with covetous pleasure, thinking privately that it would take a legion of mad wives, foul fiends, and hideous sheeted specters to rouse me once I had settled down for the night.

"I'm sure you will, too," she agreed, "but if any noise should wake you, pay no attention to it—it will be the wind. Tomorrow morning you'll not have any duties save to become acquainted with your pupils."

"I am looking forward to it," I assured her mendaciously since all I had in mind at the present moment was to divest myself of my damp garments and go to bed.

"Good night, Miss Ayers," Lady Kathleen said.

"Good night, Lady Kathleen," I responded, grateful to see the door shut upon her at last.

Yet the minute I was left alone in that vast apartment, I felt oppressed. While Lady Kathleen had been with me, I had not noticed that the firelight cast so many crooked shadows on the walls, nor had I heeded the wind which now seemed unnaturally loud as it shrieked around the corners. When a casement blew open suddenly, I could not suppress a gasp of terror and though I am not timid by nature, I had to force myself to close it. As I did, I heard an eerie wailing sob, human, yet inhuman at the same time. Someone or something seemed to be lost out there—lost in the tempestuous darkness. Impulsively, I leaned out, calling, "Can I help someone . . are you in trouble?"

Though the sounds continued, increasing in their intensity, naturally I could see nothing. Perhaps as Lady Kathleen had warned, they were only the voices of the wind, which at that moment had seized my hair and tossed it contemptuously into my eyes and mouth. I closed my casements and ran shivering to the fireplace, but after a moment I was quite comfortable and warm again. Extracting my flannel nightdress from my trunk, I prepared myself for slumber. The bed received me as gently as a loving embrace, my head sank onto pillows stuffed with down and as I had anticipated, I slept soundly the entire night.

I awoke feeling refreshed and singularly content. For the first time in my eighteen years, I was alone in a bed where I could toss and tumble to my heart's content without encountering my sister Imogen's plump form or feeling her elbow digging into my ribs. For a few seconds, I took disgraceful advantage of my new situation by rolling back and forth, kicking up my heels, arching my body and generally acting in a manner highly undignified—especially for a governess. At last, I flopped back on my pillows and lay quietly contemplating my new quarters.

By daylight, my chamber appeared even larger, for the

sun had robbed it of shadows though not, alas, of dust. I discerned more cobwebs hanging like festoons of fine lace from the ceiling and in my distaste, I saw that a large fat spider had been allowed to flourish on a beam. Her web was huge, evidently the result of many years patient toil. I considered batting it down but decided against it since I am humane of nature even toward spiders and snakes, which, if they harm no one, have a right—so it seems to me—to live out their alloted span.

Yet I could not help wondering at the negligence of the O'Hagans or their staff of servants. My questions in that regard were soon answered, for there was a small tap at my door and before I could answer, it was thrust open, revealing a winded young woman. She fixed me with a choleric stare. "Imagine," she panted, "putting you all the way over here in a room that's not been opened since Finn McCool was a lad! It's a hard time I had finding you, indeed—up the stairs and into passages I'd not seen in all my life."

"I—I'm sorry," I said apologetically.

She grinned at me. "Oh, you're not to blame. No doubt it's a wise precaution on Lady Kathleen's part for all it's so far from the schoolroom."

"Precaution?" I echoed.

Her eyes grew evasive. "Oh, it's that little Master Brian— a limb of Satan, he is—always up to tricks, but you mustn't mind him. There's not a particle of harm in him, yet."

I could not like the way she pronounced the word "yet." It seemed heavy with sinister significance, but anyone less sinister than the girl speaking to me I could not imagine. Of medium height, she had a bony face with a high knobby forehead and earnest blue eyes. Her mouth had a humorous quirk about it and I liked her immediately. As I stared at her, she turned and bending down picked up a tray on which reposed a teapot, cup and saucer, a pitcher of milk, and a bowl of sugar. Approaching my bed, she set down the tray. "Timothy will bring up your hot water for washin'," she informed me, "an' I'll just poke up the fire a bit. Would there be anything else you'd be wantin'?"

I shook my head. "Nothing, thank you," I said, looking at the tray with pleasure. I had never had my morning tea in bed.

"You'll have a bit of difficulty finding the main hall, I'm thinkin'," observed the girl.

"Oh, yes," I said quickly, "can you tell me how to get back?"

"Well, you're located in one of the four towers of the Keep," she began, "so it's not so difficult once you get the picture in your mind—the schoolroom and the main hall being midway betwixt and between them all. When you come out of your room, turn left and walk all the way down the corridor to the stairs—go down the stairs one flight, take the door on the landing, right, cross that corridor and you'll find a pair of stairs that'll lead you to the entrance hall, where one of the footmen will show you to the schoolroom."

To insure my safety, I repeated her instructions carefully, trusting that my really excellent memory would support me. It did.

"Right the first time," marveled my handmaiden, who was called, she soon informed me, Agnes, having been hopefully named after a saint, a precaution on her mother's part that had not assisted materially in giving her a holy character, she added with a giggle.

As soon as Agnes left, I had my tea and some delicious buns with jam. Then another knock announced Timothy, a tall, freckle-faced lad of sixteen or so who was carrying two heavy water cans, which he placed in the bathroom, then backed hastily out of the room, grinning and turning beet-red for some reason. Alone once more, I jumped out of bed, tended to my ablutions and donned one of my black gowns. As I was struggling with the fastenings, I heard the sound that had startled me on the previous night—the sobbing and wailing under my window. A chill of foreboding ran up my spine; but I could not resist the temptation to look. Approaching my window, I thrust open my casements and leaned out. A beautiful sight met my eyes—my tower faced the sea and below me, I saw its waters now serene and blue under an unclouded sky. Then the wailing began again and, turning, I gasped in horror, for there, perilously close to the cliff's edge, stood a slim young girl with wind-tossed russet hair and some sort of a disgracefully transparent white garment whirling around her thin body. Though I only saw her features in profile, she appeared to be uncommonly lovely, but that impression was quickly swallowed up in my concern for her safety.

"Be careful, miss," I yelled, "you'll fall."

She did not heed me but only continued her keening.

"Miss!!!!!!!" I screamed, "do take care, please. You're far too close to the edge of the cliff!"

Slowly, she turned toward me and I saw that her eyes were green as grass. She raised them to me, "You'll not be giving *me* a warning?" she said in surprise.

"I don't want you to fall—and if you'll tell me what's troubling you, perhaps I can be of some assistance."

"You—are offering *me* assistance! You'll not be an O'Hagan connection, then?"

"No—no relation, but please . . ."

"And yet you can see *me*," the young woman said.

I began to think her mad. "Certainly I can see you. I have excellent eyesight. Please come away from the edge of the cliff! You'll fall to your death."

"Sure an' it's passin' wonderful," she exclaimed. "In three hundred years, I've not seen the like!"

Then, of course, I was positive she was a lunatic. "S-Stay there, m-miss," I stuttered, "I'll get help." I hurriedly buttoned my dress and dashed out of the room. In my concern, I forgot Agnes' directions and ran down a corridor right into an immense cobweb. Shrieking in disgust and terror, I brushed its nasty clinging filaments out of my eyes and turning back, I fled down yet another corridor—more dust rose in the air causing me to sneeze and the passage was so dark that I could not see where I was going. In desperation, I flung open a door, hoping that the light from a window would brighten my way. As I stood on the threshold, however, an absolutely fiendish yell resounded in my ear.

"And what are you about, young woman?" demanded an irate voice from the darkness.

"I—I don't know where I am!" I cried.

"Obviously," remarked my unseen host waspishly, "or you wouldn't come stumbling in here. No one in his right mind enters this room!"

Instead of increasing my panic, his observation piqued my curiosity and, steadying myself, I took note of my surroundings. As the windows were tight shut and curtained, I could see very little—however, a single beam of sunlight creeping through a crack in the shutter did outline some bulky shapes which I took to be chairs and a highboy, but the occupant of the chamber still remained invisible. "Where are you, please?" I demanded.

"It's a question I've oft asked myself," growled my host. "Neither heaven nor hell but a little bit of both for my sins, I expect."

My panic returned, for the words were certainly those of a madman. I felt abused. Jane Eyre had only to deal with one lunatic whom she had not met until midway in her stay at the mansion. I had been in O'Hagan's Keep only a single night and had already encountered two—it seemed a superfluity. Wasting no more time in reflection, I sped out of that shuttered chamber and heard the door slam violently in my wake. Racing down the hall, I came to a full stop at a blank wall.

"I must be calm, I must . . ." I told myself and stood quite still, waiting for my pounding heart to resume its regular steady beat. Then I forced myself to walk slowly back along that shadowy corridor. When I reached the hall, I took another turning and, by great good fortune, discovered a staircase leading to the main part of the castle. As I emerged into the great hall, I found Dimitri O'Hagan standing by the hearth talking to a young footman. He looked at me in surprise.

"Good heavens, girl, have you fallen into a dustbin!?" he asked, brushing the remains of a cobweb from my hair. He gestured to the servant, who grinned and left us.

"A dustbin! A madhouse!" I cried indignantly. "At least I might have been warned about . . ." Then I remembered the young woman on the cliffs. "Oh, dear—oh, please, you must help her!"

"Help whom?" Dimitri was obviously startled.

"There—there's a young woman under my window. I—heard her sobbing and then . . ."

"A young woman," he repeated. "What does she look like?"

"Red hair and green eyes, but that's no matter, she——"

"Oh," he interrupted, looking relieved, "one of the maids, no doubt."

"Maid or no—she's in deadly peril!" I exclaimed, "and daft as well!"

"Daft?"

"Please," I stamped my foot, "while we stand here talking, she'll have fallen over the cliffs—and even if she does not—she'll catch her death—dressed as she is—in—in nothing but her—er—shift and that thin as gossamer." I felt a blush creep up my cheeks.

"Red hair, green eyes, and sobbing in her shift," Dimitri said slowly. "You saw her? You actually saw her?"

"Please!" I pressed his hand beseechingly, "please—won't you help her before it's too late?"

Though he returned my clasp warmly, he did not budge an inch. "Well, by all that's holy, you saw her and you not even an O'Hagan!"

I thought that I understood his hesitation. "You—you needn't think I—I'd tell people about her. I'm sure that all old families have their share of—demented persons—but certainly you ought to take better care of her and—and that other poor man." Indignation tinged my tones. "The idea—leaving the poor creature all by himself in that dark room. I wouldn't treat a mad dog in such a manner!"

"Other—poor man," echoed Dimitri. "Who else did you meet, pray tell?"

"Aren't you going to rescue that girl?" I demanded feverishly.

"She's beyond my helping her," Dimitri returned, "and . . ."

"If you won't go, I shall—she'll be drowned!" I tore my hand from his grasp and started back across the hall, but he leaped after me and caught me by the shoulders, holding me fast. "Miss Ayers, hear me—she was drowned —three hundred years ago!"

I am sure my mouth fell open. "You're mad too," I gasped, trying to free myself from his hold. "It's too much. Three in one morning!"

Dimitri shook me slightly. "Who else did you meet?"

"I don't know. He made no more sense than you. Let me go!"

I heard a rustle of silk and a shocked gasp. "Dimitri," Lady Kathleen exclaimed, "again—and after all you promised me!"

Feeling his grasp loosen, I wrenched myself free and turned to find Lady Kathleen shaking her head sadly, her large blue eyes disapproving and her mouth set in a firm hard line.

"Kathleen," Dimitri exclaimed, "listen to me."

She raised a protesting hand. "Please—no explanations. I have eyes."

"She has seen Meg!" he yelled.

"Meg?" Lady Kathleen stared at him in consternation. "Impossible!"

"She did—she described her perfectly and what's more, I've the feeling she ran into old Fitz, too. I told you not to put her in that wing."

To make what became a long argument and a longer explanation shorter, I was informed that the young woman and the man were respectively, Meg, the family banshee, and Fitzroy O'Hagan, a deceased member of the clan. The one plagued the family with predictions of disaster—having been dishonored by an O'Hagan, and the other haunted the room where he had been murdered some two hundred years before. Both, I was assured, were harmless and all Irish castles had their specters. Since English parsonages were not lacking in these nonpaying tenants, I could, in all honesty tell them that I was not in the least disturbed by them. "Indeed," I concluded reasonably, "I'm considerably relieved that neither is mad."

Dimitri gave me a long look. "Well," he said finally, "not in the ordinary sense of the term, anyway."

"Dimitri, you must not tease Miss Ayers," reproved his cousin.

"I wouldn't dream of it, Kathie. I can't remember when I've met a young woman I respect more."

A shade of alarm glinted in Lady Kathleen's eyes, then she shrugged, laughed and said, "I think it's time we introduced Miss Ayers to her pupils."

I started guiltily. I had forgotten all about my reason for coming to O'Hagan's Keep. "Please," I said hastily, "I am most eager to make their acquaintance."

The schoolroom, on the floor above the great hall, proved large enough, at first glance, to accommodate a whole tribe of children. As we came in, I heard a child weeping loudly and saw a little girl holding a doll. Lady Kathleen hurried to her side. "Darling Marra, now what's the matter with you?"

"L-Look, Mama," the child thrust the doll at her and I saw that it had been shockingly mutilated—an arm and leg torn off and its stuffing pulled from its chest. "B-Brian d-did it, Mama," Marra wailed.

Used as I was to my brothers' onslaughts on such toys

as came our way, I still felt repelled by this wanton destruction. Evidently, Lady Kathleen was similarly affected, for she made a smothered exclamation and immediately drew her little girl into her arms.

"Now, now, macushla," she murmured soothingly, "we'll get you another doll."

"I—I want this one," sobbed her daughter.

Lady Kathleen pushed back her tumbled blond curls with a gentle hand. "You don't want Miss Ayers to see you crying like a baby—and you all of eight years old, now do you?"

At that, the child raised her head and looked at me for the first time out of blue eyes shaped like her mother's. "You—you're the English lady?" she inquired.

"Miss Ayers," corrected Lady Kathleen.

"Miss Ayers," Marra repeated, wriggling from her mother's grasp and staring curiously up at me. I noted with satisfaction that she was very pretty.

"Yes, I'm Miss Ayers and I am very glad to make your acquaintance," I told her cordially.

Marra curtseyed but before she could respond, I heard a rush of footsteps and found myself confronted by one of the most beautiful and angelic little boys I had ever seen. He looked, in fact, almost as saintly as the pictures of those horrid children in the instructive books Papa forced us all to read on Sundays—the ones who were always doing good deeds, being misunderstood or mistreated by their elders and died young, forgiving all.

"Brian! Nasty Brian, I hate you!" shrilled Marra, glaring at him.

"Brian?!" I gasped, looking at Lady Kathleen for confirmation. Could this be the limb of Satan mentioned by Agnes?

"Brian!" echoed a frightened voice in the hall. "Master Brian, where are you?" A plump middle-aged woman in a dark blue uniform hurried into the schoolroom. "There you are!" she exclaimed. "How many times have I told you—you're not to go running off like that!"

"Molly," Lady Kathleen shook her head and indicated me, "Miss Ayers has arrived."

"Molly," Marra cried, "look what Brian did to my dolly!" She thrust it under his nose. "Look, you bad, bad boy."

He stared at it blankly. "How'd it get all torn, Marra?" he asked.

"It wasn't done on purpose, Miss Marra," Molly said, "you know that, now."

To my amazement, Marra nodded and sighed, "Yes, but . . ."

"Miss Ayers," Lady Kathleen arose and, taking me by the arm, walked with me into the hall, "I—I'd meant to explain to you about Brian but that bit concerning Meg put it clear out of my mind. He—he's a dear little boy, as you can see, but he's subject to—er—spells of—uh—temper, and then—he's rather destructive."

"Yet he's allowed to remain with the other children?" I asked.

"Oh, yes, he's quite harmless during the day. It's at night that these outbreaks occur—he has bad dreams. We hope he'll outgrow them. However, you need not be concerned. In the schoolroom, you'll find him good as gold."

I had noticed that during our conversation she had avoided looking at me and I had the feeling that she had not told me everything about Brian, especially when I remembered what Agnes had said. Yet, if I was startled by this information, I was not really disturbed. After all, a small boy of seven might be able to wreak destruction on a doll but there was little he could do to me. Thus, I was able to reassure her that Brian's tempests would not daunt me. "I'm used to small boys," I added. Those words had no sooner left my tongue than I felt a sharp familiar sting on my ear and whirled to find another of the species grinning up at me, both hands behind his back. About ten years of age, he had a snub nose, large ears, round hazel eyes, and a semitoothless grin.

Unthinkingly, I leaped at him, wrenching a wad of paper from his hidden hand. "I'll have none of that, sir!" I commanded.

"Kevin," exclaimed Lady Kathleen, "now what have you done?"

"He's shooting spit-balls at me, Lady Kathleen," I told her, taking him by the ear. However, I released him very quickly, "I—I am sorry. This is Kevin, you said. Your son?"

At that moment, Kevin made a dash for the school-room only to be halted by his mother, who grabbed him.

"Miss Ayers," she said grimly, "you have my permission to treat this miscreant as he deserves!"

I glared down at him and he grinned up at me. In spite of his mischievous tendencies, I liked him. However, it would not do to let him know it. "He is a very naughty boy," I said coldly, "and he deserves a good spanking, but I shall suspend punishment this time. In the future, I shall not be so lenient."

"You hear that, Kevin?" Lady Kathleen questioned sternly.

"She's got yellow eyes like a cat," Kevin observed.

"Kevin!" groaned his mother.

"Cats have green eyes," I corrected him, "owls have yellow eyes."

"Owl-eyes, owl-eyes, you've got owl-eyes!" he chanted happily and leaped into the schoolroom.

"Ach, they do not behave so badly as a rule," sighed Lady Kathleen, evidently believing that she was speaking the truth.

"It's natural they'd be excited—a stranger in their midst and all," I told her. "They seem delightful and I am sure we shall get along splendidly."

"You're a good sport, Miss Ayers," Lady Kathleen said gratefully, "and you must not be afraid to discipline them— I leave them in your hands."

We went back into the schoolroom and after showing me where my books and supplies were, she and Molly left me alone with my pupils. The minute the door closed on them, the children ran to me talking at once. I put my hands to my ears.

"One at a time!" I begged.

Though they tried to obey me, I was still hard put to answer their multitudes of questions.

"You're English, aren't you?"

"Where'd Mama and Papa get you?"

"How old are you?"

"You aren't like our other governesses—you're much prettier."

"Can you play croquet?"

"I can play chess, can you?"

"I hate arithmetic."

"I'd like to learn how to play the Irish harp, can you teach me?"

"I like spiders. I have one in my pocket in a box, do you want to see him. He's all hairy."

"I like dogs better. I want a dog—a puppy."

It was Brian who had voiced this wish and I looked at him in surprise. "You don't have a dog?"

"Dogs always run away from here," Marra told me solemnly.

"Yes," assented Kevin with a sigh.

I was surprised—there was so much space in which to exercise a puppy. At home, we always had several.

"I'll see if I can get you one," I promised.

The morning passed quickly. Since I did not have to begin their lessons, I decided to find out their preferences. Unanimously, they told me that it was history—Irish history. The mere mention of Ireland's glorious past and their eyes glowed. It did not matter that I knew little or nothing about that particular subject—they quickly became my teachers. I heard about ancient High Kings, about the copper-decorated palace of Tara, about a brave man named O'Neill and another called Desmond. My heroes, on the other hand, were their villains. Sir Walter Raleigh, he who had flung his cloak in the mud for a queen to step upon—he, who had gallantly gone to his death in the reign of her hardhearted successor—his name was anathema to these children—even little Brian glared at the mention of it. There were other enemies—all of them British, and the more I listened to them, the more my wonder grew that the O'Hagans had hired an English governess. Surely, I thought to myself, there was some mystery here. However, before I could ponder much upon it, Molly came to tell me that my pupils and I would be expected to join the family for the noonday meal.

After we had freshened ourselves, we went down to the dining hall. We were the first to arrive, for which I was pleased because it gave me the opportunity to examine my surroundings more closely. It was a beautiful room, paneled in dark wood and hung with magnificent tapestries. There was an Oriental carpet on the parquet floor and overhead a bewigged Bacchus courted Ariadne in a pastoral approximation of Naxos. The long table was covered by a heavy damask cloth set with cut crystal goblets and ornate silver. A silver bowl in the middle of the table held a profusion of late autumn flowers, and looking through the windows, I saw more flowers growing

44

in lovely ornamental gardens. Impulsively, I moved closer to them, staring out at clipped lawns and patterned paths; extending along a distant walk I saw a hedge topped with topiary animals—strange fanciful beasts, some with wings and some with curling tails. Delighted, I clapped my hands, then quickly clasped them, remembering that as a governess I must be dignified.

"Oh," I said without turning around, "I've never seen such beautiful gardens!"

"How fortunate for us that they should meet with your approval, Miss Ayers. If they did not please you, would you cast a spell on them?"

Startled, I turned to find myself alone in the room save for a slight man, who surveyed me from the threshold. My first impression of him was that he was all gray—certainly the hue predominated in his silvery hair, slate-colored eyes, and broadcloth suit. Yet he did not give an impression of age—his pale skin was unlined and his eyes were full of a youthful fire. As I stared at him, his lips twitched. "You are a witch, aren't you?" he asked.

"Witch!?" I exclaimed.

"Conan," Lady Kathleen swept into the room and fixed accusing eyes on my companion, "are you saying something outrageous to poor Miss Ayers? Come—leave her alone, please."

"Yes, Conan, mind your manners," advised a tall bronzed man, who followed her.

"But Patrick," protested the man called Conan, "you know I have no manners."

"That's the truth, sure," Lady Kathleen nodded, "though I'd not be boasting of it. Miss Ayers, this is my husband, Patrick, Lord Concullen—and this," she glared at the man in gray, "is his graceless cousin Conan. And what did I hear you call Miss Ayers?"

"I merely asked her if she were a witch." Conan's eyes gleamed with malicious humor.

"What is this talk?" A tiny black butterfly of a woman fluttered in from the hall and clutched nervously at Lady Kathleen's arm. "Do we have witches, too?"

Lady Kathleen shook a reproving finger at Conan. "No, Tanya—only in Conan's fevered brain. Please—let me present Miss Ayers."

The dark little lady, introduced as the Princess Tanya O'Hagan, looked at me out of Dimitri's eyes, as she said with an even more pronounced accent than that of her son, "You—are a witch?"

"No, Tanya, no, no, no!" boomed Lord Concullen. "It's only one of Conan's doubtful jests."

"It's not a jest," Conan protested. "What, then, does one call a young lady who sees spirits?"

"Unfortunate?" Dimitri had joined us.

"No," Conan responded seriously. "I'd not call it unfortunate but ..."

"That is quite enough, Conan," interposed Lady Kathleen.

"But I must know," persisted the Princess, "did you actually speak to the banshee?"

"I—exchanged a few words with her," I mumbled, feeling extraordinarily foolish. My humiliation increased as a burst of laughter followed fast upon my remark.

"Just in the way of greeting, now," grinned Lord Concullen.

The Princess did not smile. She raised clenched hands, "Oh, why does she not leave us in peace? Why does she stand beneath that window and weep? What new doom will she bring us?"

"Maman," Dimitri flung an arm around her, "you are being Russian!"

"But, Dimitri," she began.

"Shhhhh ... no tragedies at lunch, I beg you."

As I was puzzling over this interchange, Lady Kathleen said, "No doubt you must be wondering how we are all related, Miss Ayers?"

"Well, yes, I have been," I told her dutifully.

Lady Kathleen then proceeded to tell me that the O'Hagans, as a clan, were wonderfully close and generally lived under the parental roof. Patrick, Conan, and Dimitri were the sons of three O'Hagan brothers—Sean, Lord Concullen, Michael, and Dion, none of whom had survived to see their children reach their majority. There had also been an Ian O'Hagan, the elder brother of Conan and it was he who had fathered Brian and his sister Fiona.

"You're forgetting David, Kathie," Dimitri had evidently been listening to her recital. "David is the son of my father's sister, Nora. She married a man named Fallon and went to live in Dublin."

"And—Fiona," I inquired, "does she live here, too?"

"Ah, she does that," he smiled. "She'll be joining us soon."

"Will she be one of my pupils, too?"

"There's nothing you can teach my niece," Conan said behind me.

"And that is why she's so spoiled," Lady Kathleen sighed, "because her uncle and all her big cousins dote on her. Where is she, I wonder?"

"No doubt she is sitting in front of her mirror as usual," replied the Princess tartly.

"Maman, you are being unjust," Dimitri told her quickly. "Our Fiona is not vain."

She gave him a glance in which was mingled bitterness and concern. "No, she is an angel, of course. Like her mother before her."

A trace of alarm passed over Dimitri's face. "Sleeping dogs," he muttered at her.

"Dogs?" she questioned, an odd expression in her eyes.

"If our 'angel' does not soon join us, she must partake of ambrosia rather than clam broth—for I am not going to wait lunch for her," Lady Kathleen said firmly.

She held to her decision and five minutes later, we sat down to table without the mysterious Fiona. We were midway through the fish course when she joined us. As my back was to the door, I did not see her enter but I heard her high, light voice.

"Oh, dear, am I late? I hope you'll forgive me."

"Fiona, not another new gown! How you do indulge her, Conan!" expostulated Lady Kathleen.

He shook his head, "I've nothing to do with it. She has her own money to spend."

"So that is why she is late," I heard the Princess mutter to Dimitri, "little peacock!"

"Shhhhh, Maman."

In another second, Fiona had walked around the table and I had my first glimpse of her. I looked at her in amazement—in spite of her cousins' flattering words, I had not been prepared for such loveliness. She was quite the most beautiful young girl I had ever seen—even including myself—and by appearance, far more qualified to be a heroine than I. Certainly, she had all the features that the romancers of our day find irresistible. About sixteen, she was of medium height with long pale golden ringlets, artlessly—actually artfully—arranged so that they appeared naturally loose and flowing. Equally artfully artless was her attire—a froth of dimity and lace, carefully chosen to display as much of her white skin as it was modest to show, hugging a tiny waist and flaring over an immense crinoline which she had learned to manipulate so that it seemed to conceal not ordinary limbs and feet but air—so gracefully did she glide across the floor. Her eyes were deep blue, her mouth full and rosy, her cheeks faintly and—I am loathe to admit—naturally pink. She shared that angelic expression I had noticed in her brother, and I wondered if she might also possess his less saintly proclivities. I doubted it. In fact, though I quite ached to find something to dislike about her, I could, at that moment, discover nothing. She had a sweet manner, a lovely smile and appeared quite unself-conscious—to the point of sticking out her tongue at Marra, who had made some rude remark to her, and tweaking Kevin's hair—gestures that proved her very much the child despite her fashionable attire.

She was also too young to be subtle and it soon became obvious to me that she had eyes only for her Cousin Dimitri, whom she faced across the table—he sat next to me. It was with something of a chill that I realized he was by no means immune to her charms and that his dark eyes had become unusually brilliant as they dwelt on her. I grew even colder, when on looking at the Princess, I found that her face was almost distorted with hate, suggesting that she was possibly jealous of Dimitri's regard for Fiona.

"Miss Ayers," Conan drawled, "please tell us more about your adventurous morning."

Inwardly I sighed but I kept my features carefully bland as I replied, "Oh, it was not so much adventurous as instructive—I learned a great deal about Ireland." I sent a smile toward my pupils, who sat at the far end of the table.

"Now, now, Miss Ayers," Conan reproved, "you know very well what I mean—in addition to Meg, you met old Fitz, too."

A knife dropped from the Princess' fingers to the floor as she stared at me in alarm. "You—*saw him,* too?"

"Now, Maman," Dimitri clasped her hand comfortingly, "surely you are not frightened of Fitz—he's harmless enough, poor soul."

The Princess shook her head. "But what manner of woman have you introduced into this household?" she cried fearfully. "I have lived here for twenty years and I have not seen either the——"

"Tanya," Lady Kathleen interrupted, "Miss Ayers might have a special vision but——"

"It is called," Conan defined, "a gift."

"Perhaps," Fiona fixed her large blue eyes on me, "Miss Ayers is actually an O'Hagan in disguise."

"Certainly not!" Dimitri exclaimed. "Miss Ayers comes from a respectable family."

A mock-angry chorus greeted his sally, and to my surprise, the beautiful Fiona glared at me fiercely, an expression contrasting so strongly with her previous serenity that it startled me. Yet, a second later, she smiled so prettily that I thought I must have imagined it. "Dimitri," she said in a soft voice, "am I not respectable, then?"

"Entirely, my sweet," he said hastily.

"Entirely, my sweet," Conan echoed dryly.

She made a little face at him. "Do not be nasty, Uncle Conan," she chided.

"To you, my love, never!" he protested. Yet it was obvious to me that he did not share his family's admiration for his beautiful niece. I could, however, take no comfort in that, for I was even then aware that Conan O'Hagan had little admiration for any of his fellow men. I wondered briefly what experience had warped his nature but soon forgot him in listening to the table talk. It had now shifted to Irish history—a subject that fascinated my employers as much as it had their children. Indeed, I could see why, for through their pungent anecdotes, their dead heroes lived again and truly seemed more gods than men. As the talk continued, I thought I discerned a pattern in it—as though they were trying to tell me that Ireland, with her ancient civilization, her warriors and saints, her magnificent medieval universities, her inspired poets and scholars, owed no debt to England but, indeed, boasted a far greater heritage. Again, I wondered why they had introduced an inexperienced English governess into their household. Even their hospitality toward one who was their economic if not their social inferior* became suspect. In my hasty decision to leave my family I

* My own people, if not rich, are well-connected. My great-great-aunt was a baroness. (L.A.)

had not given much thought to the location of my employment and, as I have said, Mrs. Costello's words had made little impression on me. Now, I was again forcibly reminded of the ever-present enmity between our countries and wondered wildly whether I was to be held hostage, a situation not unique in novels but, I hoped, rather more unusual in real life. However, I prided myself that I would be equal to the situation, for unlike the average heroine, I was not lacking in ingenuity. In fact, when I was younger, my sister Oriana and I had enjoyed many a laugh at the predicaments in which these young ladies had been placed by their creators. We had even invented a game in which we provide alternate solutions to the difficulties they encountered. For instance, one of them, imprisoned in a dungeon cell, we had refrain from substance until she was thin enough to squeeze through the bars. In those days, we had known little about female anatomy. Surprisingly, all these thoughts flitted through my mind while I was eating, a fact I modestly attribute to the lavish repast rather than to my quickness of intellect. Certainly, if I was meant to be victim or heroine—two roles interchangeable in the literature of our day—I would not be able to starve myself free of my cell.

At length, our lunch ended. The children, I was told, would not return to the schoolroom immediately—we would go for a walk. I found this to be a daily routine imposed by Lady Kathleen, who had a theory that exercise aided the digestion. Her stipulation was most welcome to me as I longed to see more of the grounds, especially the gardens. My pleasure increased when Dimitri offered to accompany us.

"I presume," he said omnisciently, "that you want to see the gardens, Miss Ayers—and it's easy to get lost in them—they are surrounded by woods."

"I'll come with you, too," Fiona quickly.

"In that pretty new gown?" Lady Kathleen protested. "That's no walking dress. Go some other time, child, when you're wearing something suitable."

Fiona pouted, then shrugged and laughed. "As usual, Aunt Kathie, you are far more sensible than I. I'll go change, at once."

"And we must wait for you?" Dimitri demanded. "No, for Miss Ayers has only a limited time."

"But Dimitri," she begged, "please—it will take only a few minutes."

"Good heavens, such a to-do over a walk," marveled the Princess. "One would think the child was imprisoned in her room most the day—instead of being allowed to ramble as she chooses—God knows where!"

She walked away and I saw Fiona dart an angry glance after her. Then she shrugged, "Very well, I shall not go—since everyone seems to be in league to prevent me." If the words were petulant the smile that accompanied them was singularly sweet, and five more minutes passed while Dimitri hastened to assure Fiona that she was not the victim of a cabal and to promise her another stroll later in the afternoon. Possibly, he would have expostulated even longer had not Marra pulled at his coat impatiently.

"Oh, do come on, Dimitri, if you're going with us. Who cares about old Fiona, anyway?"

I had to hold my hand stiff at my side to keep from patting my little pupil fondly on the head. Fiona, however, whirled over to her and slapped her sharply on the arm.

"You speak when you are spoken to," she flashed.

"Fiona, what's the matter with you!" exclaimed Lady Kathleen.

"You're not my teacher!" flamed Marra, "and what's more I think Miss Ayers is much, much prettier than you are. So there!"

"So do I!" Kevin said.

"I do, too," Brian added.

To my surprise and relief, Fiona merely laughed. "You're only silly little children. Who cares what you think!?" Her blue eyes dwelt on me speculatively. "And she *is* very pretty."

"That's more like you," Lady Kathleen said, as she left the room.

"Yes, well spoken, Fiona," approved Dimitri.

"Thank you, miss, you are very kind," I murmured, wishing privately that she had shown herself to be less generous.

"Not 'miss,' " she told me gaily. "Call me—Fiona, and I shall not address you as Miss Ayers, either. Why you're hardly any older than I am. What's your given name?"

Marra answered for me, "Jane."

"Jane?" echoed Fiona, *"Jane* Ayers?"

"Mama said it should be," giggled Marra.

"I thought it was Lucinda," Dimitri said.

"It is," I admitted regretfully.

"Oh, and do they call you Lucy, for short?" Fiona asked.

"Yes, usually."

"Lucy it will be, then," Fiona nodded. "I will see you later, Lucy." She ran out of the room.

"Do let's go," begged Mara.

"Are you ready, Miss Ayers?" Dimitri smiled at me.

Upon my signifying that I was, we all went out a side door into the gardens. They had looked beautiful from the window—as we strolled along graveled pathways and through arbors covered with flowering vines, I found them even more lovely. Especially impressive were the trees—great copper beeches, fir trees heavy with cones, and others for which I had no name. Some of the flowers and plants had come, Dimitri told me, from Russia.

"So Maman would not be homesick," he explained. "Here—this, too, is from the country of my birth." He pointed to a strange stone bird.

"You were not born in Ireland?"

He shook his head, "Until I was fifteen years old, I lived in Kiev. Its accent still clings to my speech—for all I have tried to eradicate it."

"But it is a pleasing accent," I said.

"Not to me—I am an Irishman, after all. And trust is difficult enough to win even——" he broke off. "Let us say, Miss Ayers, that if I am to have any sort of accent at all, I should prefer a brogue."

I wondered why, but I did not feel I could ask him without appearing far too forward. After all, we had known each other less than twenty-four hours. Consequently, I said merely, "I still like the way you speak. It is very unusual."

"It is that," he agreed wryly. "The wise Dr. Pangloss might have called it the worst of all possible worlds—Irish and Russian together. It has given me a most peculiar disposition."

"Cousin Dimitri!" Marra who had run on ahead of us with the others, came dancing back. "May we race to the edge of the woods?"

"That far but no farther, mind you," he said sternly.

"We'll be very careful," Marra promised, skipping away.

"Woods? Are we so close to them?" I asked.

"They are close to us," he sighed, "and coming nearer each year—each year they annex another piece of this land. You'd never believe it, Miss Ayers, but these gardens used to be the wonder of the countryside."

"Used to be? But they are still so beautiful."

"No, come and I'll prove to you that they are wild, desolate, and overgrown." He quickened his pace and indeed, the farther we walked, the more tangled and unkempt the foliage became until it did actually merge with the forest.

"Can nothing be done to prevent this?" I inquired. "You have gardners. I saw them."

"And they—have many tasks," he said. "Many tasks." Though his words were innocuous, I could see that they had a meaning to him that was not apparent to me. A look of bitterness was reflected in his dark eyes and suddenly I was reminded of Jane's Mr. Rochester with his brooding and enigmatic silences—except that to my mind Dimitri was much the more attractive of the two. I wondered if I, so early in our acquaintance, dared consider him the hero of my story. Possibly . . . even though the presence of Fiona was daunting, even to one of my optimistic nature. It was, I thought, unkind of fate not to have provided her with mousy hair or at least a spotty complexion.

"Miss Ayers!" he said loudly.

I jumped, "Yes, Mr. Roch—uh—O'Hagan," I stuttered, hoping he had not noticed my slip.

"Did you hear what I said to you just now?"

"Uh—about the gardeners. Indeed it is a shame that . . ." Under his frowning gaze, I subsided.

"You were not listening to me, I fear. Very well, I must repeat myself. You'll no doubt be called upon to take the children for other walks about the grounds and possibly you, too, will want to go for some solitary strolls. I must ask you to confine these peregrinations to the hours before sunset. I would not want you to stray into the woods by error—they can be very dangerous at night."

"Oh, I know," I said, thinking of the fog I had encountered the previous evening.

"You know?" He stared at me very intently. "What do you know, Miss Ayers?"

A mysterious element seemed to have crept into the conversation and I longed to ask a few questions of my own but dared not. Instead I said simply, "There was a dreadful fog here last night, but I suppose I must accustom myself to them—since we're so close to the sea."

Some of his tension departed. "Yes, we do have bad fogs here."

"I love the sea, though," I hastened to add, fearing he might think I had been complaining. "At least I love to look at it," I amended, remembering my late voyage.

"Yes, it's . . . what's that?" He stiffened, listening.

In a second, I heard it, too—a soft, rustling sound in the bushes behind us, as if some animal were creeping toward us. Then, suddenly, a thicket was parted by two white hands and Fiona, graceful as a fawn, leaped out, laughing. She had changed into a plain green gown that was just as becoming as her frills.

"Dimitri!" she cried, "did I startle you?"

He laughed. "Ah, the fleet-footed Fiona, I knew you'd be joining us soon."

She pouted. "Oh, you believe you know everything, do you not?"

Unexpectedly, he frowned. "No, I do not believe that."

"You're quite right," she nodded. "There's much I could tell you if I chose—but I do not choose." Her eyes glinted, full of an elfin mischief.

"I'm not asking you to betray your secrets, Fiona." Dimitri was smiling again. "Come, shall we continue our walk?"

"Oh, dear," I said, "I wonder where the children are."

"They're on ahead, I hear them," Fiona told me.

"Do you? I don't." I could, indeed, hear nothing.

"I have very sharp hearing. There—they are laughing. Listen."

"You *are* a little peacock," Dimitri said, "always showing off . . . sharp hearing, however, is not an accomplishment—it is a natural gift."

"If you are going to be prosy, Dimitri, I shan't walk with you." She tapped him playfully on the arm.

"I'd better join the children," I said, trying not to envy their camaraderie.

"Oh, yes, you must pay attention to your duties, dear

54

Lucy." If her words were reproving, the smile that accompanied them was merely teasing. I chose, however, to heed her.

"At once," I said and started off.

"Hold, Miss Ayers," Dimitri laughed. "Do you know where you're going?" He came up to me. "We'll all join the children."

Putting himself between Fiona and myself, he refused to quicken his steps and we strolled leisurely along the path. He continued to point out various features of the gardens—such as a rhododendron planting, a sundial, and a half-ruined temple nearly overgrown with ivy and other shrubbery. I was fascinated by it.

"It must be ancient!" I exclaimed. "And yet the Romans never came to Ireland, did they?"

"No, but a French architect did," laughed Fiona. "Our great-uncle Michael had it built in this manner."

"Ruined temples were very popular toward the end of the century," explained Dimitri.

"Oh," I nodded my head knowledgeably, "the Gothic revival—and do you have a grotto, here, too—with all sorts of unnamable horrors within?"

"A grotto!" Fiona stared at me. "Why would you think we had a grotto here?"

"We have no grottoes," Dimitri produced an exaggerated sigh, "only that harmless little temple."

"Oh," I laughed, "a haunted castle should have at least one grotto."

"I will tell that to Patrick." Dimitri smiled. "Perhaps he will build one in the sea caves."

"In the sea caves!" Fiona said sharply. "We'd get all wet." She shivered. "I hate those nasty caves."

Dimitri stared at her in surprise. "Why should you hate them, pray?"

She seemed uncommonly grave. "Because they are cold and—horrid."

"Sea caves?" I queried.

"Below the castle," Dimitri said.

"I should like to see them," I said.

"No," Fiona fairly shot the word at me, "no one ever goes into them. Except—the sea."

"No," Dimitri agreed, "they're dark and dangerous and besides they smell most dreadfully of fish."

"You've been in them?" I asked.

"Once when I was little. Danny and I went exploring."

"And—what did you find?" Fiona's voice quavered.

"Nothing . . . we didn't get very far—but why should you be so afraid of them, child?"

"I don't like the idea of holes in the earth that lead to —to hell!" Her great eyes were dark and shadowed.

Foolish as her words were, I shivered, then I laughed and said lightly, "I don't think hell's gates are so close."

"How do you know?" she asked tensely.

"Because she's not a silly little girl," Dimitri told her.

"Nor am I." Fiona's voice was grave.

"Well, then—you have an overactive imagination," he said. "I suppose," he added, "we'd best find the children— it's nearly time for afternoon lessons."

"Oh, dear," I exclaimed, "I hope I haven't lingered too long."

"I'll take the blame for that," he reassured me with a smile.

"Miss Ayers . . . Lucy," Fiona smiled at me, too, "do you suppose that I might come to the schoolroom this afternoon? Aunt Kathleen said I may work on my French with you, if I choose?"

"I should be delighted," I told her, hoping I sounded convincing.

"Well, Miss Ayers, you are to be complimented," Dimitri said, "I never heard Fiona ask for lessons before— usually she'd do anything to avoid them."

Fiona made a face at him. "I must improve my French. I intend to go to Paris one day and how shall I converse with all the French gentlemen unless I am proficient in the tongue."

"You'd do far better to say nothing and merely smile at them," returned Dimitri, though whether he was being gallant I could not know, for I had not yet determined the depth of her intelligence.

I ran a little ahead of them to call the children but I received no response and unlike Fiona I could not hear them.

"Oh, dear, where are they?" I cried.

"Do not worry, Miss Ayers," Dimitri said easily, "they're probably playing in the graveyard."

The graveyard! Naturally, there would have to be an ancestral plot on the grounds—we came to its gates short- ly afterward and it proved as picturesque as any I had ever read about. Indeed, it would have been a poet's delight, for there were the hemlock and the yew trees, the marble urns and the ornate but crumbling tombstones. In the middle of the enclosure stood a small marble mausoleum which, I learned, had been built in the seventeenth century. It had heavy bronze doors and over them was an inscription which, translated from the original Latin, read, "Rest Thou, O Perturbed Spirit." Underneath this message was carved the Pentagram, its five points outlined in gold. I would have asked Dimitri more about this edifice had not a sudden burst of childish laughter reminded me why I was there. Going in the direction of the sound, I found Kevin and Marra sitting on a broad flat stone making a daisy chain. Brian, however, stood apart from them, near a great marble urn in which a few flowers had been placed. They had evidently been there more than a day because they were wilting and faded.

"Oh," breathed Fiona beside me, "how quickly flowers die."

Looking at her, I saw that she had grown melancholy again. She was certainly a creature of moods. Then, as she approached nearer to the urn, she stamped her little foot. "Brian, was it you who put these weeds in Mama's vase?" Reaching in, she tweaked out a small bunch of wildflowers and tossed them disdainfully to the ground.

Brian's reaction was immediate and startling; he launched himself at his sister in a furious headlong manner. Instantly, Marra and Kevin jumped up and ran to him, each grabbing one of his arms.

"Brian, no!" Marra commanded.

Fiona, instead of being alarmed, as I was, by an outburst that seemed almost maniacal, merely laughed and said, "Oh, Brian, don't go into a pet."

Dimitri pulled Fiona back. "Why do you goad him?" he chided. "You know his disposition."

She shrugged. "If he wants to bring flowers to Mama's tomb, let them be pretty roses or chrysanthemums—not old weeds from the field."

"They aren't weeds!" Brian wailed. "And Mama would have liked them!"

"You know nothing about it," retorted Fiona. "You never even saw her."

"Fiona!" Dimitri actually shouted, "that is enough." He gave her a little push. "Go along now and stop tormenting

Brian!" Loosing her, he strode back to us and, lifting the child in his arms, he hoisted him onto his shoulders. "Let's go for a ride!" he smiled up at the little boy.

His good spirits restored, Brian shrilled, "Giddup, giddup, horsie," and dug his tiny feet into Dimitri's ribs with a will.

Dimitri only laughed. "He's a regular little Cossack! I'm fortunate he's not wearing spurs."

"Does he have a pony?" I asked, as we walked to the gate.

"No," Dimitri shook his head.

"I want a dog!" Brian said.

On hearing this, Fiona, who had been waiting for us at the gate, burst into laughter. "A dog?" she questioned.

Dimitri frowned at her. "That's enough, Fiona."

Remembering my promise, I persisted. "Why shouldn't the children have a dog?"

Marra, who was skipping at my side said, "They just won't stay with us."

"No," Kevin nodded, "they always run away. I don't know why."

"We have very bad luck with animals here," Dimitri agreed.

Again, I was startled by Fiona's laughter which seemed both inexplicable and inappropriate, especially as she refused to explain what had amused her.

A silence descended on us, then, and lasted throughout our walk back to the castle where, to my confusion, we entered by yet another door which took us through a labyrinth of small passages to the main hall.

Once indoors, I discovered that I had yet another half hour before I commenced lessons and I occupied the time in trying to fix an easy route to my room. After consultation with Agnes, whom I discovered in the dining room, I established a set of landmarks distinguishable by day and night and, on my third attempt, found my way with ease. I was returning from this exercise when I met Lady Kathleen.

"You're rather winded, my dear," she observed.

When I had explained what I had been doing, she commended my ingenuity. "It's easy to get lost in the castle," she sighed. "So much of it is shut off these days. Why, there are parts of it I've scarcely seen myself. The O'Hagans built to accommodate troops of soldiers and retinues of servants. Why, there was a time when we sheltered a whole village. Nowadays, our staff has shrunk to a mere handful. I do not doubt that our ancestors are turning in their graves—those that sleep in them, I mean." She laughed. "It's no use trying to hide our family skeletons—or spirits—from you."

I, too, laughed. "They do not really disturb me—spirits. They are harmless, after all."

Like a cloud sailing over a placid lagoon, a frown shadowed Lady Kathleen's serene eyes. "Still, I shouldn't encourage them too much, if I were you, my dear. Some-how, I do not think we were meant to be on—uh—familiar terms with the dead. We have trouble enough dealing with the living."

There was a look of distress on her face, and I wondered what unhappy secret had prompted this bit of advice. Gently, I reassured her, "I shall be careful, Lady Kathleen."

She smiled. "I'm sure you will, my dear. And I might add that I'm delighted at the way my children seem to have taken to you."

Thanking her, I returned to the schoolroom where I found the children waiting for me. Though they wanted to continue my introduction to Irish history, I told them firmly that it was my turn and set them to copying an alphabet by way of improving their handwriting. We were in the midst of this lesson when Fiona came in. She carried several books with her which proved to be two French readers and a grammar. Leaving my other pupils at their exercises, I started working with her. I found that she had a tolerable pronunciation and could see that she had also been given a thorough grounding in grammar.

"Who was your last instructor?" I asked her.

Fiona sighed, "Miss O'Rourke."

At the mention of the name, Marra lifted her head and gave Fiona a reproving look. "You know we're not sup-posed to speak about Miss O'Rourke, Fiona," she said.

"I did not speak about her," Fiona flared. "I merely said that she taught me French. That's not speaking about her."

Though I quite burned with curiosity, I quelled it. "Marra, continue with your lesson. Now, Fiona—we will converse in French."

For the next half hour, we conversed on such diverse

subjects as a visit to the Jardin des Plantes and a night at the Opéra; then, thinking I had devoted enough time to Fiona, who was not, after all, my main concern, I excused myself and began to ask the children questions about geography and botany. On the whole, I found them well informed. Too, they proved to be intelligent and even diligent, though several times I had to restrain Kevin from wriggling about too much in his chair and launching paper projectiles at Brian. Brian, on the other hand, was docile and studious. If I had not caught a glimpse of his temper, I would not have believed him capable of anger. When our hours of study finally ended, I decided that I did not mind teaching at all, and we parted, tolerably pleased with each other.

As I started to leave the room, however, Fiona, who had been sitting apart, watching me, came up and put a restraining hand on my arm. "Miss Ayers ... Lucy," she began tentatively, "I do hope that we can be friends." Before I could answer, she continued hurriedly, "I have been so lonely since Deirdre left us. We were really very close."

"Deirdre?" I repeated.

"Deirdre O'Rourke," she clarified. "I do not know why we shouldn't mention her. It's silly, and honestly I do not believe that Dimitri should be blamed for her disappearance. Servants will chatter so!"

It would have taken considerably more control than I possessed not to question her further. "Miss O'Rourke—disappeared?"

Fiona nodded. "One night. Katie, one of the housemaids, said that Princess Tanya had her packed off because she did not approve of the interest Dimitri was showing her. Personally, I think she grew bored with the country and decided to return to Dublin. She was always talking about city life. And truthfully, Dimitri didn't care about her at all. He just likes to tease people. He used to tease Miss Haydon, too."

"Miss Haydon?"

Fiona nodded. "That was the governess before Deirdre. She also ran away one night, but I think it was Brian's tantrums that drove her to it. He can be very difficult, as you saw this afternoon."

"Yes," I said faintly, over the lump that seemed to be

lodged in my throat. "It—it's quite a coincidence—both of your governesses—leaving so—suddenly."

Fiona shrugged. "It's very lonely here. There are no balls—no social gatherings—only the family. That's why both Nora Haydon and Deirdre set their caps for Dimitri—even though I warned them both that he has promised to marry me—when I am eighteen."

The lump in my throat threatened to cut off my breathing. "Has—he indeed?" I said faintly.

"Oh, yes," she nodded. "We've been in love for ages. That's why Aunt Tanya does not like me." She giggled. "But she wouldn't dare send me away."

"You seem very young to have been in love for—ages," I commented.

Her laughter vanished. "I may be young," she said, "but I know what love means. Dimitri is mine, heart and soul—and I am his." She spoke with such intensity that, against my will, I found myself believing her.

"Well," I told her, "you must hurry up and become eighteen then."

"Oh," she sighed fretfully, "it does take such a long time. You're eighteen, now—or even older?"

"I shall be nineteen in November."

"Oh, I should love to be that old—then I should have been married to Dimitri for a year. He is twenty-five."

"An old man," I managed to laugh.

"No, he's beautiful," Fiona exclaimed. "But enough of my darling Dimitri—since Deirdre has gone, I am, as I told you, without anyone with whom I can talk. I do hope you'll be my friend—my bosom friend?"

With a weak smile, I answered, "I—will try to be."

"Oh, good," she said, evidently unaware of my hesitation. "That means we can tell each other everything and we shall never, never be parted—except by death!"

Since that implied a longer tenure than I had in mind, I contented myself with a restrained, "I hope we will be very good friends, Fiona."

"Oh, yes, yes, yes!" she agreed joyfully, flinging her arms around my neck and kissing me rapturously on the cheek. She left me after that, disappearing down one of the corridors. Thankful to be alone once more, I felt the need of fresh air. I went downstairs and out into the gardens. It had, I noticed, grown misty again and the declining sun was already partially obscured. Yet the land-

*61*

scape was sufficiently attractive to entice me. In my previous excursion that day, I had been more interested, I admit, in listening to and looking at Dimitri. Alone, I could concentrate more perfectly upon the wealth of ferns and flowering plants that met my eyes at every turn. I could wish I had seen the gardens before autumn had touched them with its blighting fingers, but still, the reds and golds were beautiful and I could almost wish that there were someone to see me as I wandered among them, for with my golden coloring I could not help but know that I must have created a pretty picture—a modern pastorale, as it were. Indeed, my interior visions of myself actually succeeded in obliterating the earlier panic I had felt at Fiona's confidences.

Alas, pride, as Papa is fond of saying, goeth before a fall and I, my gaze on the turning trees and sylvan vistas before me, was unmindful of my steps and where they led me. Suddenly, however, I felt a clutch at my skirts and found that I had become entangled in a bramble bush. As I stopped to free myself, I was aware that it had grown much darker and, staring around me, I realized that inadvertently I had wandered into the woods. Quickly I yanked at my skirts and in that moment, I heard it—a noise, as if something were moving in the bracken. Peering into the gloom, I could see nothing, but at that moment a clump of bushes stirred and a small tree quivered as if a body had brushed against it quickly in passing. Some animal—some wild animal—had sensed my presence and was after me! Overcome by panic, I turned and dashed blindly away, only to be brought up sharply by a great oak which had reared itself in my pathway, or so it seemed to me. As I dodged around it, the sounds behind me grew louder and closer. My pursuer was gaining on me! I dared not look back but as I ran, I heard heavy breathing and a sort of snarl.

"Oh, God help me," I wailed, and then I ran into ye another tree.

"Miss Ayers . . . Miss Ayers, is that you?" I heard someone call.

"Yes," I screamed loudly, "and—and there—there is something . . ." In that moment, my voice froze in my throat, for I saw two gleaming eyes peering into mine. In that misty darkness they were horridly bright and I could actually feel their malevolence. Caught by their evil glitter, I was as powerless to move as a rabbit fascinated by a stoat. They came closer to me, but in that moment Dimitri plunged into view.

"Miss Ayers, what are you doing here?"

"The eyes . . . the eyes . . . ?" I cried.

"What . . . ? Where?" He looked about him.

"There . . ." I pointed a quivering finger and then let my hand fall to my side, for I saw nothing. "They—they're gone!" I felt myself swaying.

"Don't faint!" he commanded harshly.

Indignantly, I replied, "I have no intention of fainting. I never faint!"

"Good," he said, taking me by the arm. "Watch your step!" he added, as I nearly stumbled.

Finally, to my relief, we came back to the gardens and I sank down on the grassy sward, saying quickly, "I am not fainting. I am just sitting!"

He ignored my explanation. "What were you screaming about?"

My panic returned. "There—there was something—following me. It—had eyes."

"Eyes . . . ?" he echoed.

"Horrible shining eyes—like—an—owl—or a cat."

"Probably," he said coldly, "it was an owl or a cat."

"It was bigger—much bigger and—and—I know it meant me harm." I shuddered.

"Probably you imagined it," he said infuriatingly.

"I didn't," I returned indignantly. "It was—I——"

"And what made you go in there when I warned you to keep out of the woods after sunset?" he interrupted.

"It's not after sunset," I reminded him, "it's just foggy."

"Don't argue!" he ordered.

I was so annoyed by his attitude that, forgetting my terror and fatigue, I leaped to my feet. "I am going to my room!"

"Good," he approved and then he smiled and, reaching forward, he pulled my hair.

I glared at him. "Sir!"

"You don't want to go into the house looking like a dryad," he said, holding up a branch of leaves which he had evidently extracted from my curls, "even though the colors are very becoming to you."

I am sure that I blushed and of course I had to laugh, too.

"That's better," he approved. "You should always smile. You have such a pretty mouth."

"Dimitri!" Lady Kathleen suddenly appeared on a path. "What are you doing with Miss Ayers?"

He sighed, "Nothing, Kathie, I assure you."

Under her chastening glaze, he left me and I went back into the hall and up to my room, reaching it without mishap. It was not until I had settled myself at my desk and opened my diary that I thought of the eyes again. I wished that I could dismiss them as pure imagination but I had seen them and I knew that they belonged to someone or something that had threatened me in a manner I dared not even name to myself. In that moment, I decided that I would never set foot in those woods again—not even in broad daylight. I wrote that resolution in my diary, underlining it twice, and then—as I laid down my pen, yet another fearful memory arose in my mind—Fiona's revelation about my two predecessors. Had they, too, strayed into the dark woods and . . . It was a chilling idea but even more chilling was the thought that Dimitri and/or his mother might have been instrumental in their departure. But it was Dimitri who had warned me—Dimitri who had rescued me—Dimitri, who would eventually marry his cousin . . . at that moment my thoughts became very confused, not to say chaotic. I sighed. In all the novels I had read, the heroine generally became involved in a dark mystery associated with the man she loved or, at least, liked. Following her as she attempted to extricate herself and her lover from his entanglements had been exciting to me as a reader. In real life, however, I discovered that the mere thought of being similarly menaced caused me to suffer goose bumps, a lump in my throat, and palpitations, none of which symptoms did I welcome.

To return to my initial day at O'Hagan's Keep, you would have thought that the few remaining hours before bedtime would have been without incident but no, as I was blotting the pages of my diary, Timothy came to tell me that I would be expected at dinner.

To say that I contemplated another gathering of the O'Hagan clan with reluctance would be an understatement. I was tired, confused, and frightened, and though I had been reasonably satisfied with the gowns Imogen had made for me, I feared they would be sadly lacking in style and freshness—especially when contrasted with Fiona's

64

probably extensive collection of dresses, each more dazzling than the last. Yet it did occur to me that Dimitri had probably seen most of them unless she, in common with Queen Elizabeth, wore them only once. In spite of her wealth, I doubted that she would have been allowed to be that profligate. If my musings seem a trifle tart for one who had just acquired a bosom friend, I must plead that I was as yet unused to this idea. At home, I had not sought for friendship outside my large family circle. I had quite enough companionship as it was, and until Oriana married, we had been fast friends. As my senior, she was unconcerned by our possible rivalry. Imogen, only ten months younger than I, positively hated me and I must say that she failed to evoke any tender feelings in me— her hair being of a red shade that clashed strongly with mine. I am afraid, therefore, that despite Fiona's openhearted offer, I still considered her a rival whose presence I did not welcome in company with the opposite sex, even supposing Dimitri to be beyond my aspirations. I know I lack generosity but a life in which I had been forced to share nearly all of my possessions had rendered me particularly protective of those which I could call mine—they being only my youth, my beauty, and my charm.

It did not take me long to choose which of my three dinner gowns I would wear. First impressions being important, I decided upon the amber silk that complemented my tawny hair and my golden eyes and hoped I would create an overall effect of loveliness rather than be singled out for the style of my garments alone. The large fulllength mirror returned an image which would have satisfied me completely, if it were not for the thought of Fiona. Feeling discontented, I walked into the hall and in my concentration on my appearance, or the lack of it, I took a wrong turn and found myself in another dark unfamiliar corridor. With an annoyed sigh, I started back and nearly bumped into a very tall, thin, pale man in black. He put out a hand to avert our collision and I fear I moved away from him with more haste than decorum for never had I felt flesh so chill.

He seemed unaware of my reaction, for he smiled cordially enough and observed in a deep voice with a trace of Irish lilt, "Ah, what vision falls upon mine eye?"

Having no compulsion to flirt with him, I answered prosaically, "I'm the new governess, sir."

"The—new governess," he echoed and I thought I discerned a flicker of disapproval in his dark eyes, which were brilliant even in the half-light.

"Ah, Miss Ayers." To my surprise, Dimitri, somewhat out of breath, joined us. "I was afraid you might take the wrong turning so I came to fetch you. Good evening, Uncle Fingal. May I present Miss Ayers, who just arrived from England yesterday."

"She—is the Englishwoman?" inquired his Uncle Fingal in disdainful tones.

"Yes, sir, I am," I retorted proudly.

"We should go down to dinner," Dimitri said quickly. "Come, Uncle Fingal, David will be joining us tonight."

"David? Ah—then I shall come."

I supposed that had David not been expected, he would have supped in his chamber rather than sit down to table with an Englishwoman.

I wished that I could think of something intensely patriotic to say about my country, but unfortunately nothing except a few Shakespearean quotations came to mind and though I was an educator, I did not want to seem a bluestocking all the time, so I contented myself with ignoring Fingal O'Hagan and smiling at Dimitri, though I daresay my expression was wasted in the dark. When we emerged into the lighted hall again, however, Dimitri stared at me with considerable appreciation. "How lovely you look tonight!"

In spite of all I knew or did not know about Dimitri, I was again charmed by his personality and intrigued by his appearance. Consequently, I decided to be demure and looking down shyly, I murmured some disclaimer—an effect immediately spoiled by his Uncle Fingal, who snorted loudly and growled:

"Speak up, speak up. In my day, Englishwomen were known for their clarity of diction if for nothing else."

His use of the words "in my day" startled me more than his implied insult, for he appeared only a few years older than Dimitri—thirty-six or seven at the most.

I am sure that Dimitri caught my confusion, for he said, "Come, come, Uncle Fingal, no need to talk as if you're a hundred and ten—and furthermore, there is certainly no need for you to be so discourteous to Miss Ayers. Come now, apologize to her!"

The words that Uncle Fingal muttered might or might

not have been an apology, I did not care. Assuming him to be one of those misogynistic eccentrics common to many old families, I decided to ignore him. However, as we traversed the twisting corridors, I found his presence increasingly disturbing. He seemed to carry with him a chill I could actually feel. I was considerably relieved when we finally arrived in the dining hall.

As we entered, we found the Princess chatting with Lady Kathleen. Both ladies looked elegant. Lady Kathleen was arrayed in a rich purple velvet gown, and though the Princess wore her accustomed black, its heavy satin folds swirled over a huge crinoline while diamonds gleamed in her décolletage and in her hair.

"Maman!" Dimitri exclaimed. "How lovely you look!"

She turned quickly, but as she faced us her tender smile faded and a look of terror came into her eyes. I saw her hand rise quickly to her forehead—she, too, was making that gesture I had witnessed the previous day. I heard a pained gasp beside me and saw Uncle Fingal stiffen and turn alarmingly rigid—evidently, he was in the throes of some sort of spasm. I wondered if he suffered from fits, a malady which might explain his pallor. Then, as he regained his composure, he looked reproachfully at the Princess.

"Madame," he whispered in a constricted voice, "would you please refrain from doing that?"

"Fingal," the Princess had recovered her equilibrium, "I must ask you to forgive me. It's just that in my country . . ."

"Your country, Princess, is Ireland and not the fringes of Outer Mongolia as I need hardly remind you after your decade among us. Certainly, I join you infrequently at best and——"

"Fingal," Lady Kathleen said gently, "good evening and welcome."

His stern features relaxed into a smile as he bowed over her hand. "Good evening, my dear Kathleen. And where might your husband be this fine night?"

"He'll be joining us soon."

"And David?" pursued Uncle Fingal. "Is he in good health?"

"Hale, hearty, and whole," she replied.

"Ah, excellent, excellent," Uncle Fingal said. "I have high hopes for the lad."

"You'll find him worthy of them," Dimitri told him.

"Yes," Lady Kathleen nodded, "Patrick has heard very good reports of David. His friends are most pleased with his work."

It seemed to me that there was another deeper meaning concealed in their words, but then my common sense overcame my romantic invention. Obviously I had allowed the strangeness of my surroundings to affect my imagination. Mentally, I took another look and found myself in the midst of a pleasant family gathering, which at that moment was increased by Fiona, a vision in ivory silk garlanded with tiny rosebuds on vines of green moiré ribbon. As I had feared—or rather anticipated—she looked exquisite. Trying valiantly to keep in mind that we were bosom friends, I smiled cordially at her and was, in turn, greeted exuberantly.

"Good evening, Lucy. How lovely you look!"

I smiled and returned her compliment but soon realized she was not listening. She was, instead, staring at her Uncle Fingal and I noticed that some of the radiant color had drained from her cheeks.

"Good evening, Fiona," he said punctiliously.

"Good evening, Great-Uncle Fingal." She curtseyed and produced a small, set grimace, evidently intended as a smile.

"How is your dear little brother Brian?" inquired her great-uncle solicitously.

"Well!" To my surprise, Fiona almost snapped the word.

"And now we have a new governess," he said. "An Englishwoman."

I detected a faint breath of sarcasm in his intonation and wondered at it. I wondered the more at the fury I glimpsed in Fiona's eyes.

"We have decided to be bosom friends, haven't we, Lucy?" Moving to me, Fiona put an arm around my waist and I was surprised to feel that it was almost completely rigid.

"Have you?" Uncle Fingal's eyes narrowed. "Have you indeed?"

A little defiantly, I said, "I do not think your uncle approves your choice, Fiona—feeling as he does about Englishwomen."

Unexpectedly, he smiled. "On the contrary, Miss Ayers,

I wish every Englishwoman might have Fiona for her bosom friend."

Strengthened in my opinion that the man was a hardened misogynist, I smiled. "Indeed, sir, I count myself very fortunate."

Fiona smiled brilliantly. "I, too," she asserted, glaring at him.

At that moment, this puzzling and uncomfortable conversation was interrupted by Dimitri, who, looking appreciatively at Fiona, remarked, "Ah, a vision from heaven!"

"Dimitri!" protested Uncle Fingal, wincing.

"*Heaven?*" giggled Fiona. "Do I really look as if I came from *heaven?*"

Dimitri frowned. "Enough, Fiona," he commanded and, turning to his uncle, he put a conciliating hand on his arm. "I'm sorry, sir." Then, smiling at me, he added, "I think, however, that I may safely say that Miss Ayers has arrayed herself in the gold one finds at the ends of rainbows."

Uncle Fingal snorted and turned away from us, and Fiona, summoned by Lady Kathleen, also left us. Dimitri smiled down at me. "Well, Miss Ayers, are you sorry that you came to O'Hagan's Keep?"

I considered him seriously, thinking again how much his dark looks appealed to me. "I've not had much time to be glad or sorry, I've been here only a day."

"Only a day?" Dimitri said. "It seems much longer. Indeed, I feel as if I'd known you for . . ."

"Dimitri?" The Princess, standing immediately behind us, had evidently been listening to our conversation and her voice was heavy with warning. Dimitri stiffened and, almost curtly, he turned from me and moved to his mother's side.

Her glance of angry reproof had sliced through me like a sharp knife. I could well understand her reasoning. A Russian aristocrat would scarcely approve her son's dalliance with a mere governess. With a chill, I remembered Fiona's remarks about my predecessors and had a sudden vision of Dimitri smiling at those two young women as he had smiled at me and . . . before I could continue these melancholy reflections further, David Fallon came in with Lord Concullen and Conan. All conversation ceased as his family surged forward to give him a fond greeting.

He was a tall, handsome young man who bore a striking resemblance to Lord Concullen except that he lacked his repose. He had a taut, watchful air and it seemed to me that he vibrated with excitement much like a tuning fork, which being struck retains the hum long after the impetus has disappeared. Though I had no foundation for my belief, I was positive that he had not come to O'Hagan's Keep merely to pay respects to his family.

"Are we ready to go—hunting tomorrow," I heard him ask Lord Concullen.

"Yes, quite ready," his cousin replied. "We'll pick up the hounds at O'Riordan's."

"Ah, that's a fine pack, if I remember correctly," he said, his eyes gleaming. "Good at sniffing out foxes or wolves."

"Wolves?" I gasped, involuntarily. "Surely not in this forest?"

I found David Fallon's eyes on me. "And who might you be?" he asked.

I felt my cheeks burn. "I—I did not mean to speak out of turn—I . . ."

"This is Miss Ayers, David," Lady Kathleen led me to him, "and it's my own bad manners that I've not introduced her. She's from England. Miss Ayers. Mr. Fallon, our cousin from Dublin."

"Delighted, Miss Ayers," he bowed slightly. "Well, you've come a long way and you—are afraid of wolves?"

"I suppose I would be," I returned, "only I cannot believe that there are any left in Ireland. I've read that the last one died before the end of the seventeenth century."

He laughed. "But you must not credit all that you read in your English books, Miss Ayers. Historians are not hunters and, as a hunter, I can tell you there are enough of the beasts terrorizing our land to furnish an Irishman with a bit of sport."

"Do—they lurk in this forest?" I gasped.

"You'll find them throughout the length and breadth of Ireland." David Fallon grinned. "Now that will be something for you to tell the British, will it not?"

"David, what are you saying about wolves?" Fiona came and stood by her cousin, looking up at him with laughter in her eyes.

"Fiona," he said softly, "now how could you have become any more beautiful?"

Tacitly she acknowledged his compliment. "I am six

months older than when last I saw you." Her smile brought two fetching dimples to the corners of her mouth.

"Ah, then you'll have turned sixteen!" he answered. "I shall have to buy you a birthday gift."

"Oh, will you, David?" she cried, delighted as a child. "What will you get me?"

"Stardust and moonlight," he said.

"Silly," she giggled, "I would prefer a bangle."

"A bangle it shall be." He took her wrist and pressed a kiss on it. "Would pearls suit you?"

"Pearls and diamonds," she said audaciously, "for you promised me stardust and moonlight, did you not?"

"That I did, mavourneen, and I'll buy you the finest I can find in Dublin."

"Oh," she sighed enviously, "I wish I might go to Dublin."

"Perhaps one day, I'll take you," he returned.

She gave him a roguish look. "But that would not be proper. Aunt Kathleen would never allow me to go with a gentleman—all by myself."

"Under certain circumstances, she might," he began, only to be interrupted by Lady Kathleen's announcement that dinner was served.

As we took our places, I felt cheered by their conversation. Obviously, David was inordinately fond of his cousin, and Fiona, despite her avowed passion for Dimitri, had not discouraged him. Even now I saw her giving him coy glances from under her long lashes and displaying her enchanting dimples. I had not been hungry before, but now I found I could thoroughly enjoy the delicious viands set before me. Everyone ate with a good appetite, in fact, except Uncle Fingal, who touched neither food nor drink. No one, however, seemed at all surprised by his lack of hunger, but Dimitri, who must have seen my questioning glance, whispered to me.

"Uncle Fingal has already dined. He's on a special diet for his health and rarely joins us at dinner—but he's very fond of David Fallon."

"Oh," I responded. It was obvious to me that not only Uncle Fingal but the entire household, servants included, doted on the young man. Both men and women hung on his every remark with passionate interest, straining to catch his words, which, for some reason, were spoken huskily— his voice rarely rising above a whisper. I could, in fact, hear nothing of what he said, but I supposed him to be detailing his Dublin experiences which evidently had the fascination that city life must invariably present to the country-bred. Even Dimitri, who, this time, had been placed between Fiona and myself, had very little to say to either one of us. Though Fiona seemed content to try and listen to her cousin, I, for my part, wished he would either talk louder or desist entirely. Then, I was glad no one could read my thoughts, for surely they were not indicative of that submissive and gentle nature a governess must necessarily maintain in a household where her authority and her importance, such as they are, end in the school-room.

As is the custom, the ladies left the gentlemen to their port and, as we trailed out of the room, an explosive burst of conversation followed us and I am sure that I heard David Fallon, louder than all the others, say something about the "damned English." Naturally, I wanted to hear more but since I could hardly linger in the hall, I reluctantly followed Lady Kathleen into a chamber she had called the music room. It was located on the other side of the great hall and I entered it only to pause at the threshold, awed by its magnificence. Its paneled walls were painted ivory-white and hung with yellow silk, while over the ceiling stretched a glowingly beautiful mythological scene depicting Orpheus playing his lute to a rapt audience of nymphs, satyrs, and other woodland deities. The room was furnished after the fashion of fifty years ago—tables were set either on Grecian pedestals or on the backs of crouching sphinxes. The couches had graceful curved arms ending in lions' heads or swans' wings; the lines of the chairs were equally fluid. Set around the room were various musical instruments—a pianoforte, an Irish harp, and a lute.

"Oh," I breathed, "lovely."

The Princess smiled graciously and I learned that she had decorated the chamber, using furniture she had reclaimed from the attics. To my mind it had much more beauty than the modern predilection for the squat and the massive.

As I penetrated farther into the room, I saw that there was a cabinet in which other musical instruments were displayed, including a violin of considerable antiquity.

"That," Fiona said, as she saw me looking at it, "used to be played by dear Uncle Fingal."

"Oh, is he a musician?" I inquired.

"He used to be," she nodded. "He's out of practice now. His fingers are too stiff." I sensed an undercurrent of amusement in her speech, as if she were enjoying a highly private joke.

"These," Lady Kathleen had joined us, "are called the Pipes of Pan—as you can see they are actually fashioned from reeds."

They looked incredibly ancient to me. "How old are they?" I asked.

Lady Kathleen shook her head. "I'm not sure. One of the O'Hagans brought them back from Greece some three hundred years ago."

"They might have belonged to Pan himself," I laughed.

"No, if they had—he'd have found a way to retrieve them," Fiona remarked.

I stared at her. "Surely you don't believe in Pan!"

She looked at me for a moment without replying, then in a low voice, she answered, "There's something out there in—our woods. I've heard his music."

Lady Kathleen clicked her tongue. "And that something is Fiona's lively imagination. Silly child, you will listen to old wives' tales." She turned to the Princess. "Tanya, will you play for us?"

"If you wish," the Princess said. From another cabinet, she brought out a stringed instrument which resembled a guitar but proved to be a balalaika. She had a husky contralto voice which was a little untrue when it came to pitch, but she used it so skillfully that she turned this deficiency into an asset. I was fascinated by the music which was full of sadness and pathos. Though she sang in Russian, we had no difficulty in understanding that her song told of thwarted love, separation, and farewell. When she had struck the final chord, I caught her eye on me, but I cannot say that she really saw me—she seemed to be looking beyond me, beyond the room, beyond the time— back to the land from whence she and her instrument had come.

As silence fell upon us, we were all singularly moved by her performance. It was the Princess herself who broke it. "Kathie," she said, "it is for you to entertain us now— with an Irish ballad."

Lady Kathleen smiled and shook her head, suggesting that I might give them an English ballad instead. Since a governess must be proficient in music, I regarded her invitation as a test and, breathing a silent prayer, I chose "Barbara Allen," one of the few songs I know from memory. I suppose I sang it tolerably well but I am sure they would have applauded whether I had or not. Certainly, my performance was bland compared with that of the Princess, but then she had the leisure to perfect her musical skills. I wondered how else she had occupied herself during her ten years in Ireland. With her haunted eyes and sable garments, she was not the least of the mysteries I had encountered that day. And Dimitri's father, what had he been like? Had he resembled Patrick, too? I could imagine that he had—his golden hair and blue eyes must have indeed intrigued the Russian beauty to bring her across so many seas. I hoped that the O'Hagans had a portrait gallery. Family-proud as they were, it seemed impossible that they would not have one of considerable antiquity. I wondered, too, if the Princess had been painted at the time of her arrival in the castle—I should have liked to see her in colors.

"A penny for your thoughts, Miss Ayers," Lady Kathleen smiled at me.

"Yes, Lucy," Fiona added, "what are you thinking about—so silent and abstracted."

Startled, I realized that they were all watching me. "My thoughts aren't worth a farthing," I laughed nervously.

"I suppose we're a bit of a puzzle to you," Lady Kathleen continued. "I hope you'll become accustomed to us—for we're all pleased with you."

I smiled at her gratefully. She, at least, appeared completely free from secret woe. She was handsome, amiable, and gracious, and with perfect truth I could say to her, "Thank you, Lady Kathleen. I hope I shall continue to please you."

"You will, Lucy," Fiona told me. "My cousin has taken a real fancy to you. And as she has said—so have we all. We never expected anyone half so———"

"Fiona," Lady Kathleen's fair brows contracted, "you do prattle sometimes!"

Fiona only laughed and stuck out the tip of her pink tongue at her, then she picked up her skirts and danced over to the pianoforte. "I shall entertain you now," she announced pertly and sitting down, she performed a long and complicated run. From her expression, I would have expected some merry little song but instead she began to play and sing in a melancholy, plaintive voice, Heine's *"Die Lorelei."*

The pianoforte stood close to the tall windows and Fiona's form seemed to merge with the lengthening shadows of twilight—with her flowing golden hair and pale translucent skin, she reminded me of a creature from another world. As the haunting, evocative music filled the room, the door was thrust open and David Fallon, who had come in quickly, stopped short, staring at her. It was evident that her singing had a potent effect on him, for he stood absolutely still, as spellbound, perhaps, as the doomed fisherman of the verses.

It was not until she finished her song that Fiona saw him. A provocative little smile curled her lips and in a sweet, compelling voice, she asked, "Did you like my music, David Fallon?"

In two strides, he was at her side. "I've been on the Rhine and I've seen the rocks where the Loreleis sit," he told her, "but I've never met one until this evening."

"Oh, do you think I am a Lorelei?" she said childishly. "That's a very great compliment."

The ensuing laughter shattered the pensive mood that had, I think, claimed us all and I, pleading that I had not yet recovered from the effects of my journey, begged to be excused. Lady Kathleen assented and I bade them all good night and came out of the salon only to encounter Dimitri.

"Hold, where are you doing?" he demanded.

"It's been a long day and I'm tired."

"Will you be able to find your way or shall I guide you?"

I shook my head, "I must learn to do that without assistance," I told him firmly.

"Come, Dimitri, shall we join the ladies?" Conan and Lord Concullen had come up to him.

"Good night, then," he said and I thought I discerned a trace of reluctance.

"Good night, Mr. O'Hagan," I answered and fled. As I carefully made my way back to my chamber, I tried to subdue my chaotic thoughts.

"It's too soon, too soon, too soon," I repeated to

myself. "I've only been here a day. One cannot fall in—become attracted to anyone in a mere twenty-four hours. It's quite ridiculous. Now Jane . . ." I sighed; it was slowly being borne upon me that as a guide, *Jane Eyre* was not without its deficiencies.

When I entered my room, I found a roaring fire in the grate and my flannel nightdress on the bed. A glass of milk and an apple stood on my night table. These little attentions were most comforting and, in thinking about them, my confusion subsided. I could tranquilly record another few paragraphs in my diary, write firmly "End of my first day at O'Hagan's Keep," and go to bed.

The next morning, I awoke before sunrise, when the sky was yet a silvery gray, pierced by pins of light. Slipping from bed, I ran to the window and knelt down to look at the sea but again my vision was intercepted by the white-clad figure of the weeping woman. She caught my eye upon her and stared at me, gulping back her sobs in a very human manner.

"Can you really see me?" she demanded.

"Yes, I can," I told her. "but I know now that I really shouldn't be able to." Then, prompted by a curiosity stronger than fear, I added, "I wish you'd tell me how you came to be a banshee."

She opened her great eyes even wider but, astonishingly, she also smiled. It was a pretty smile and made her appear appealingly young and girlish. "I will that, if you want to hear," she said, "only I don't want to scream at you from this place—you must invite me up there—of your own free will."

"Of course, come up," I told her cordially.

"Of your own free will?" she asked.

"Certainly," I answered.

"You have to say it," she insisted. "Of my own free will, I invite you—Meg O'Leary. That's how you must say it."

"Oh. Of my own free will, I invite you, Meg O'Leary," I repeated.

A great gust of sea air chilled me to the bone and in front of me, smiling widely, stood the banshee. Seen at closer range she was even prettier with the pale skin that goes with red hair and forest-green eyes. She studied me with a curiosity equal to mine.

"It's the yellow eyes on her," she said at last in a low, lilting voice. "They was meant to see spirits and the like."

I shook my head. "It's Margery." I explained about our ghost.

She laughed. "It's to be commended this tolerance you have for the living and the dead—it's to be hoped you'll profit from it one day."

Evidently curious, she moved soundlessly around my room, peering up the fireplace and bouncing on my bed. "Well," she remarked, "it's a fine large room they've provided for you—and none to share it with, neither."

"Yes," I agreed, "it's a great pleasure to me after home where I had to sleep with my sister Imogen. There are fifteen of us."

"Fifteen? That's mortal many to hang on your poor mother's breast. I myself had six sisters and seven brothers. Oh, it was a big family and we were lucky when we'd not to share our beds with the pigs—my father being a farmer. Small but lusty, he was."

We exchanged understanding looks and so human did she seem that it was even more difficult for me not to believe that she was not simply a young woman like myself and one whose friendship I would have preferred to that of Fiona.

"Ah, that one," said the banshee reflectively. "You do not like our Fiona, I see."

Since I had not spoken my thought, I was understandably startled and gasped, "But——"

"Oh, I can read your mind," she interrupted complacently. "It's a knack that comes with transition; and I'll tell you true, I'm not after caring much for Fiona myself—or her mother before her."

"Why not?" I demanded.

"I cannot tell you," she replied repressively. "It's against the rules."

"Rules?" I exclaimed. "Do you have rules, too?"

"Indeed and I do," she sighed. "If it were not for the rules I should be off in the forest with those that dwell in it instead of standing beneath this cursed window howling like—like a banshee." She gave me a laughing, sidelong glance and continued, "Ah, yes, the living and the dead are bound by rules—though I probably should not tell you that. Later, I will find that there is even a rule against talking with you—though I cannot remember one. Since my—transition, I've not met a human being will speak to me. You are most unusual."

"Since we are speaking together," I said, "remember you promised to tell me how you became a banshee."

"I lost my most precious possession," she averred. Her eyes grew dreamy and she continued, "There I was, dressed in my best and bound for the fair to sell eggs, when this great black horse bars my path and who is smiling down at me but Dermot O'Hagan, one of the five lusty O'Hagan boys who were the terror of the whole village, what with their rampaging and their ruining of our girls and wasn't Brigid Casey's stomach round as a witch's pot under her apron and didn't we all know it wasn't a leprechaun as she insisted but Diarmid O'Hagan that was Dermot's older brother and him as handsome as any prince. Oh, they was all handsome and wicked, too—each worse than the last. Well, when I saw him on the horse, I was that put out. I tried to run in the other direction but he was down from the beast in a trice and, in another second, he had me by the waist, holding onto me with a grasp of iron.

" 'Are you some fairy maid?' he asked me.

" 'I'm Farmer O'Leary's daughter—and take your hand off me!' I yelled at him.

" 'You're beautiful enough to be a fairy maid,' he said, beginning to breathe deep.

" 'It's a pity I'm not, for I'd change you into a toad an' step on you!' I cried, trying to pull away.

" 'And got a sharp tongue in her head, too,' he commented.

"Well, I tried to break free from him again and I did manage to stamp hard on his foot, but though he winced, he never loosened his grasp. Instead, he lifted me high in his arms and carrying me to that great horse of his, he threw me over the saddle bow, leaped to its back, and we galloped away—with me kicking and screaming for all I was worth and the eggs all cracked on the roadside. The wicked gossoon!"

Her eyes flashed with a reminiscent fire and she fell silent.

"Then what happened to you?" I prompted.

She shook her tangled locks. "It's not fit for virgin ears

78

to hear," she sighed. "We rode past the bog and up through the forest to a quiet place where there was never a living soul to see. It was early morning when he brought me there and it was late afternoon before he let me go and rode off, laughing loudly, too. That was because I'd cursed him, you see—him and all his family.

" 'Curse away, my love,' he'd told me, 'but if the truth'd be known, you liked it as much as I did. Ah, you're a fine pretty child and a warm armful, too. If it's a son I begot this day, I'll raise him to be a lord. You bring the brat to me and see if I don't.'

"But after he'd gone, I went to a deep pool in the middle of the forest and drowned myself."

"Why?" I gasped.

"Because I'd lost my most precious possession," she said reasonably, "and my Mama'd told me that if a girl loses *that* before ever she has a ring to slip on her finger, she should die the death. Oh, it was nasty, all the water going in my nose—if I could've swum a stroke, I'd have saved myself, but I could not, so I had to make the best of it and, the next thing I knew, I was at banshee school—learning the way of it."

"You had to learn to be a banshee—in a school?" I exclaimed.

"I had that," she nodded. "It's not somethin' you pick up on your own. It's terrible hard, too. If I'd known I'd have had to be a banshee, I'd have stayed alive."

"Why did you have to be one?"

"Because I'd cursed the O'Hagans in what proved to be my dying breath—with all the water in me. Ah, I was a foolish girl, listening to my Mama that way. If I'd had half the sense . . . but it's three hundred years too late for me to repine."

"Must you be at it forever?" I asked, feeling sorry for her.

"Until the awfulest doom comes to the O'Hagans, I must," she sighed.

"And what would that be?" I inquired curiously.

"I cannot say," she told me. "It's cursed enough I've thought them any time this last century or more—it's been bad enough to keep me out here all the time—instead of appearin' at decent intervals the way most of us banshees do—but accordin' to the rules, it could be much worse and . . ." Suddenly, she cocked her head and seemed to be listening. "Ah, I'll be leaving you now—it was fine to talk with you but do not be expectin' me to make a habit out of it. I'm sure Himself will be after thinkin' up a rule against it."

"Himself?" I questioned, but received no answer, for she had disappeared and, when I went to the window, I saw her standing on her rock, sobbing and crying so hard that I decided she was making up for lost time. Try as I would, I could not attract her attention again.

Shortly after that, Agnes came in with my tea. "Och," she exclaimed, "such a smell of the sea as there is in here."

"By all rights, it should be the forest," I said unthinkingly.

Though Agnes looked her amazement, I decided not to mention my visitor. Thoughtfully, I dressed and, as I walked downstairs, I found myself wishing that Meg had told me what that awfulest doom would be.

When I entered the schoolroom, I found Kevin, Marra, and Brian highly excited.

"Papa has gone hunting," Kevin told me. "I wanted to go with him but he wouldn't have it."

"Dimitri and Uncle Conan have gone, too," Marra added, "with Cousin David."

"Well," I smiled, "that should be invigorating. What will they hunt?"

To my surprise, the children giggled and shook their heads.

"They've just gone hunting," Kevin said finally, avoiding my eyes.

I sighed. At that moment, I decided that too much mystery can be as tedious as none at all. "Will they return this evening?"

Kevin shook his head. "No, not tomorrow, either. They'll be gone a long time."

"Days and days and days," corroborated Marra.

I said, "This morning we will see how much arithmetic you know."

If they had been well behaved the day before, they were difficult that morning. Several times I had to remind them sharply to pay attention and, whenever I turned my back on them, I heard them whispering.

In a lesser degree, the same attitude prevailed among the rest of the household. Lady Kathleen was tense and abstracted, the Princess stayed in her room the greater part of the day, while Fiona, whenever I saw her, sighed often. The servants, too, exchanged knowing looks and occasionally I came upon little groups of them, talking in low voices. To me, the castle seemed lonely and dull without the men. The hours, even those I spent with my pupils, dragged, and though I was glad enough to go to my room of an evening, I found that privacy had its drawbacks. I missed the laughter and even the quarreling of my brothers and sisters. By the end of the week, I was thoroughly dispirited and actually homesick.

On Saturday morning, the children were released from lessons and I was free to do as I pleased. I had planned on asking one of the servants to drive me to the village, but when I awakened that morning, I found a heavy rain falling. Feeling more depressed than ever, I went sullenly downstairs and ate a solitary breakfast. I did not see any of the other women and imagined that they were still in their rooms. I stood for a while at the window, hoping that the rain would stop, but it only increased in intensity. Finally, I decided to go to the library and read. That prospect cheered me a little, for on my first visit there, earlier in the week, I had seen great shelves of books, many of them ages old, and some beautifully illuminated manuscripts in glass cases.

The library was located in the same wing as the music room, and as I made my way to it, I passed an open door. Curiously, I glanced in and saw Agnes busily polishing a table. "What's in here, Agnes?" I asked.

"Och," she smiled, "come and see."

I found myself in a long hall with rain-dimmed windows —the only real light came from a small lamp that stood on Agnes' table. However, even in the semidarkness, I could see that the walls were covered with paintings in heavy gilded frames. My depression vanished immediately. "This is the portrait gallery!" I exclaimed.

"It is that," Agnes agreed. "Here's the lot of them— livin' and dead."

"Oh, I wish I might see them better. It's so dark in here."

"You may have this lamp to carry," Agnes said, "as

soon as I'm done with my work. Sit yourself down on the couch, there. I shan't be long, I promise you."

No sooner had I sought the couch in question than Agnes with a grin and a flick of her cloth said, "There, I'm done. Mind you turn down the wick when you're through." She nodded at me and whisked out of the room, shutting the door thoughtfully behind her.

There were so many paintings lining the walls that I hardly knew where to start. I hoped that they were grouped by centuries, for I had more interest in the near present than in the remote past. Consequently, I started about midway and, holding up the lamp, I saw Patrick's face incongruously topped by a white powdered wig. An inscription on the frame told me that this was Oonagh O'Hagan, born 1733, died 1789. A small girl with a lace cap on her head and a goldfinch on her finger was named Marra and looked not unlike my pupil except that she had died, a child, in the year 1671. A few paces away, I was somewhat startled to see the stern features of Fingal O'Hagan, born 1733, died 1789. A small girl with a lace tume of a Restoration gentleman, he bore a very close resemblance to his descendant. Moving hastily away from him, I came upon another Patrick in a ruff, looking at me narrowly and watchfully as do all the subjects of Elizabethan portraits. I was caught by the name Dermot O'Hagan and wondered if he could have been Meg's seducer. The dates under his picture—1541 to 1565—suggested that he might have been; it also suggested that he had not lived very long after his crime. Shivering a little, I passed him, looking for the Princess and her husband. I moved hurriedly along the wall, scanning the portraits quickly, so quickly, in fact that I very nearly missed it—but out of the corner of my eye, I glimpsed it—a sweep of blond curls. Turning back, I stared in amazement, for here was Fiona. She was dressed in a white flounced satin gown, her bodice was cut very low, and in one hand she held a folded fan and in the other a bouquet of white roses. Yet, as I looked a second time, I saw that this woman was not Fiona—she was older, more mature, and her great eyes were full of melancholy and something more, an undefinable expression that unsettled me, though I could not have said why.

"That is my Mama," a soft voice breathed in my ear. "Wasn't she beautiful!"

With a smothered cry, I whirled, nearly dropping the lamp. Fiona stood behind me.

"They say we are very like," she added.

"Yes," I said weakly, "very."

"You seem nervous, Lucy. Did I startle you?"

"I—I didn't h-hear you come in!" I stammered.

"Oh, I can move softly when I choose," she said with a trace of self-satisfaction. "Would you like to see more? Let me be your guide."

"If—it would please you to do so."

"It would please me to please you," she said sweetly, "for we are bosom friends, are we not?"

I nodded, wondering if I had imagined a slight edge to her voice.

Taking my lamp from me, she moved along the wall, stopping in front of a picture. "Here is my papa."

Not too surprisingly, it was another face like Patrick's which stared back at me, under darker hair with bluer eyes. "And here," continued Fiona, "is Lady Kathleen."

It was a younger, more slender girl standing in an orchard—her white skirts swirling around her and her face shaded by a big floppy hat, but it was Lady Kathleen's frank gaze and her sweet smile. I noted that her hand rested lightly on a collie dog and again I wondered why there was no such animal at the Keep.

"Look," Fiona said, stopping in front of a larger portrait. I saw a darkly beautiful woman garbed in a rich red velvet gown, heavily stitched with gold embroidery. A mass of dark ringlets threaded with a scarlet ribbon fell to her shoulders, her full red mouth was slightly pouting, her Oriental eyes stared straight into mine, the while her hand toyed with a ruby pendant.

"The Princess!" I exclaimed.

Fiona nodded. "This was painted before she met Dimitri's father. They brought it back from Russia with them. See—the frame is all studded with precious stones."

"And Dimitri's father—is he here?" I asked.

Fiona pointed to another picture close by. "Yes—there he is. There's not much of a resemblance, is there?"

I found a young man with a slender ascetic face, thin lips and dreamy eyes. His austere features would have not been incongruous in a monk or a poet but did not suggest a man who traveled for pleasure. I wondered what had brought him to Russia.

"The servants say," Fiona whispered, "that he was a great scientist. He searched the world over for herbs and roots to distill and in the end it was one of his own potions that killed him."

A thrill of horror shook me. "He—died by his own hand."

"I did not say that," Fiona answered, "but he died. Mama was with him when it happened. It was she who heard him cry out. It was she who cradled his head on her lap and stroked his hair. It was she who closed his staring eyes—and a fortnight later, she, too, lay dead—a hunting accident, so they told me."

"A hunting accident?" I repeated. "What manner of accident?"

Fiona's eyes filled with tears. "It happened deep in the woods. I know no more about it. I was not allowed to see her—they buried her with the coffin sealed tight."

"And your father, what happened to him?"

"He—was killed in the gardens—by a wild beast. You see, Lucy, there are wolves in Ireland." She sighed. "At least in our lands—it's part of the curse that's on the Concullens."

"Curse?" I exclaimed.

"Oh, yes," she nodded. "They die young or they die hard—usually it's both. Ours is an old family and there have been many wicked people in it—so their sins lie heavily upon us, but you must never say I told you about it, Lucy. Lady Kathleen would never forgive me."

"No," I promised, "I shall say nothing."

Suddenly she shivered. "Oh, I hate it in here—have you seen enough, Lucy?"

"Yes, enough." I wished I had not heard her strange tales of death and doom. They had raised questions for which I had no answers and worse yet, they filled me with a terror for which I had no name.

On the morning of my eleventh day at the castle, I awakened with a nervousness that had nothing to do with the qualms I had been experiencing since my visit to the gallery. This was a feeling I recognized, having had it before—I suppose it should be termed a "presentiment." Generally it occurred before some unpleasant event such as the news that Mama had been strolling in her much frequented cabbage patch or that one of Papa's wealthy parishioners had died without leaving a bequest to the church fund. On two other occasions, it had presaged something more sinister, such as the deaths of close relatives. However, since I was away from home, I feared my mystic warning might involve someone at the castle. I wondered whom and hoped that if ill luck were to strike, it would not threaten my pupils, Lady Kathleen, the Princess, Dimitri, Lord Concullen, or David Fallon. I was aware that I had omitted Fiona from my so-called prayers and belatedly added her to the list. I had been trying valiantly to maintain our bosom friendship but it was rather a struggle, for at her best, she reminded me of my annoying younger sisters and at her worst, which I must admit she rarely showed, she was spoiled and sullen. I presume that jealousy also shadowed my thinking. In the eleven days I had been at the castle, I hardly ever saw her wear a dress more than once and she seemed to possess an overabundance of ornament including two absolutely ravishing pairs of diamond earrings, a garnet necklace, and an armful of gold and jeweled bangles. Papa was fond of advising us to consider the lilies of the field, which toiled not—neither did they spin, but I have always thought it a poor analogy to compare people to flowers because they really have very little in common. Lilies do not have to look modish. In fact, knowing Fiona only made the contrast in our situations the more blatant and depressing. Indeed, I had visions of myself, chained to my profession all my life—it did happen, I knew—Jane Eyre notwithstanding. Indeed, there had been an aged governess in the workhouse attached to our parish. Senile and crippled, she had sat in a corner endlessly reciting the alphabet. You would have thought that some of her old pupils might have provided for her! I am often amazed and disheartened by the discrepancies in man's estate and especially by the suffering of the destitute old and the deserted young that Papa and I used to visit in the workhouse. It seems cruel indeed that little innocent children, born through no fault of their own, must meet with such harsh treatment and be sent out to work in hard and unrewarding employments as soon as they can toddle. Thank the Good Lord that I never suffered as, say, Jane Eyre did—nor was I born to labor in a coal mine at six or ply the needle on fine embroidery in some freezing attic. I

trust that the future holds some hope for these unfortu-
nates and I tell myself that it must, for from my readings
in history, I have learned that progress, though it appears
to occupy only a sentence or two in a book, is usually a
matter of decades—even centuries, yet it does seem to be
inevitable—oh, dear, I think I am as much addicted to
asides as an actor!

My feeling of unease persisted through the morning. I
remember that I found Lady Kathleen rather preoccupied
at breakfast. Indeed, she had such a distracted air that I
wondered if she, too, had had a presentiment. However,
as I looked into the gardens, some of my forebodings left
me—it was a lovely day—the autumn sun shone bright on
the turning leaves and masses of dahlias and chrysanthemums bloomed in the flowerbeds.

"It's such a pretty morning," I commented.

"Um," Lady Kathleen returned, "very clear." It seemed
to me that she took a lugubrious view of that particular
fact.

The Princess, who had made one of her rare appear-
ances at breakfast, nodded solemnly. "There will be a full
moon tonight," she observed.

Lady Kathleen's fork dropped from her fingers and
clattered to the floor. I saw her clutch the table spasmod-
ically as she said, "There, I'm all thumbs this morning."
Rising abruptly, she left the room.

The Princess, apparently unsurprised by her reaction,
continued to drink her coffee. I supposed that I might
describe the infinitesimal movement of her shoulders as a
shrug.

In another moment, I had finished my breakfast and I
arose from the table quickly. I must admit that I had
rushed the last few mouthfuls because since my encounter
with Fiona in the gallery, I felt nervous in the presence of
the Princess. I could not help wondering if there had been
a guilty love between her husband and Fiona's beautiful
mother. Had both of them died for it—murdered by this
enigmatic Russian Medea? Certainly that would explain
her antipathy to Fiona, for what could be a worse punishment for her than to see her son marry her rival's daughter. In the absence of any real explanation of the old
tragedy, I envisioned the worst.

"Miss Ayers . . ."

"Yes, Princess!" In my own ears, my voice sounded shaken and a little shrill.

She seemed unaware of my trepidation. "You are in the habit of locking your door each night?"

"Why, not usually," I told her, startled.

"It would be advisable if you started to do so, then."

I felt that familiar lump in my throat. "Why? Has—something happened or—"

"You are in a lonely part of the castle and if anything unpleasant were to happen, no one would hear you cry out." She put her hand on my arm in the most friendly gesture I had ever seen her make. "Forewarned is forearmed, child." Giving me a fleeting, almost a shy smile, she went hastily out of the room.

Not unnaturally, I was disturbed and it took me some minutes before I could regain enough composure to face my pupils. Finally, however, I joined them. Marra and Kevin greeted me enthusiastically, but Brian was absent.

"Brian's not well," Marra said before I could inquire about him. "Molly's kept him in bed this morning."

"Oh, dear," I exclaimed, "nothing catching, I hope."

Marra shook her long curls. "He's often sick. Mama says he has a delicate constitution."

I was quite concerned, for even in eleven days I had grown fond of him. He was a delightful child, full of imagination and curiosity. The numerous questions he asked me displayed a keen mind—in all, he was a pleasure to teach.

"I will go and visit him after classes," I said.

"No!"

"No!"

I stared at the children in surprise, for their protests had been voiced almost simultaneously and they both looked apprehensive. "No? Why not?"

"We never see him when he's sick," Marra told me solemnly.

"Nobody does," Kevin agreed, "not even Mama. Only Molly stays with him."

"But if it's not contagious . . ." I began.

"He'll be back with us in a week," Marra said.

"Four days," corrected Kevin, "it usually takes four days."

"It usually takes four days!" I echoed. "Has this illness occurred often, then?"

"I think it happens most every month," Kevin said.

"Yes," Marra nodded, "it does."

I must say that I felt most confounded—I could think of only one—indisposition that occurred every month and certainly it would not be likely to affect a little boy.

"Well," I said, "if I cannot see him, I shall still ask Molly how he is. But it does seem a shame that he's not allowed to have any visitors. Time must hang very heavily on his hands."

When our morning lessons were over, I went upstairs. All the children's rooms were on the third floor, Brian's being located in a tower and reached by a winding stair. It had a heavy oaken door that swung on great iron hinges and reminded me forcibly of a prison portal. I tapped tentatively and heard nothing. I knocked again, hard enough to bruise my knuckles, and then I was startled by a low threatening sound almost like a growl—it seemed to come from behind me. Turning hastily, I saw nothing. In another second, the door opened noiselessly and Molly peered out, an anxious look in her eyes.

"Who . . . Miss Ayers—what would you be wanting?" she gasped.

I hesitated, mainly because I heard a panting and whimpering coming from inside—I also heard the rattle of a chain. "You—you've got a dog in there? A fierce dog, too, from the growl I heard. Now I've always been in favor of Brian having a puppy, but not when he's ill."

"Oh, miss," Molly's face turned red and she seemed to choke, "there's no dog in here . . . you—you're hearing things. Please, you'd better go downstairs—it's near time for lunch, is it not?"

"But can't I see little Brian—it's hardly fair to shut him away from his playmates if he's not contagious. I came from a large family and we always found that companionship . . ."

"Miss," Molly interrupted, a harried look in her eyes, "please, I know what I'm doing. I've had the care of Mr. Brian since he was a babe in arms. Now—he'll be better in a few days and then he'll be back with you at his lessons."

Again, I heard the panting and the dragging of the chain; it seemed to be coming nearer the door. I strained to see through the crack but Molly's large person was in my way. "You have got a dog in there!" I accused. To my indignant amazement, Molly slammed the door in my face and I heard a bolt slide into position.

"Molly!" I cried furiously. "Molly!"

"Lucy, it won't do any good. You may as well come down." I turned so quickly that I nearly fell down the stairs. Grabbing the rail convulsively, I found myself looking down at Fiona, who stood below on the landing.

"Come," she said in a low voice and walked back toward the other end of the corridor.

Wonderingly, I followed her. "Your—brother," I began.

"They won't let you see him until he is well again," she spoke over my words. "He won't be well again until the moon is on the wane."

"The moon!" I exclaimed.

"Shhhhhhh." Fiona put a finger to her lips. "Come with me to my room—we can talk without being overheard."

I assented gladly, for though she had visited with me in my chamber, I had never been invited to hers. It was located in a hall that ran parallel to that given over to the other children and I must say that I gasped when she opened her door. It was a bower for a Sleeping Beauty or for a Cinderella who had attained her Prince.

The walls were paneled in white wood and the ceiling was draped in white silk, rising to a peak in the center over an elaborate Venetian glass chandelier. An Aubusson carpet lay beneath my feet and the furnishings were also French—authentic Louis XV—with white and gold carved frames and satin cusions. A dainty French clock ticked on a white marble mantel and over the mantel hung another portrait of her mother, evidently painted when she was younger and even more like her daughter. Delicate Dresden figures sported on tables and the bed was hung with lace curtains and covered with a matching spread.

"Oh," I gasped, "how exquisite!"

"It is well enough," Fiona shrugged, "but this is what I like. Look." She led me toward the windows which I noticed had been extended to the floor, and opening them, displayed a small balcony. A mischievous gleam appeared in her blue eyes. "When I was little, I used to climb down that tree into the garden." She pointed at a large tree growing close to the rim of the balcony.

"But that's dangerous!" I exclaimed, looking down at the garden some three stories below.

89

"Not if you're careful." She came back into the room. "Mama had the balcony built—this used to be her bedroom. I was born here and so was Brian."

At the mention of Brian, I remembered why I was there. "What were you going to tell me about him?" I demanded. "What has the moon . . ."

"The full moon," Fiona amended. "Some people, Lucy, become distracted by the bright moonlight. Brian is one of them. It's a sickness. Mama suffered from it, too. But I—fortunately—am free of that contamination."

"You—do not mean that—that he is moon-mad?" I whispered.

"Something like it," Fiona nodded, "but you mustn't tell anyone I told you. No one knows that I know. They think it would upset me—but as you see, I bear the burden easily enough."

"But Fiona," I asked, "if no one told you—how do you know about it?"

Her eyes widened and then narrowed. "You are very astute, are you not, Lucy? Well—I told you I used to climb down into the garden when I was little? One night, when Brian was only two, I did, and saw him running around in the moonlight—two of the gardeners caught him."

"Is—there no cure for him?"

"He will, I think, become less troubled by it when he is older. Mama did."

I shook my head. "Poor child."

"Poor child!" Fiona echoed, twirling around suddenly like a Morris dancer at a county fair. "He's not a poor child. Or at least, he wouldn't be, if they'd leave him alone." She laughed at me. "Lucy, your mouth is wide open and you look like a dying trout on a riverbank!"

"Fiona!" I returned hotly, "that is not the sentiment I should expect from a—bosom friend!"

She giggled. "If I were not your bosom friend, Lucy, my love, would I have entrusted you with all these dark secrets? Anyway, you know that I was only teasing." She whirled to the door and pulled it open. "You'd best go down to lunch before they wonder where you are."

"Aren't you coming?"

"No, I shall be a little late. Make my excuses to Aunt Kathleen, won't you?"

"Very well." As I turned away, her door closed so

loudly behind me that my ears rang. I could not imagine why she had slammed it but she was in an odd, restive humor that day. However, as I hurried downstairs, I found myself thinking less about Fiona than her unfortunate brother. It was then that I recalled Agnes' explanation as to why I had been put in the other wing of the castle and too, I remembered the Princess' enigmatic warning. Like a questing finger, I felt a chill travel the length of my spine. To a healthy mind, even the hint of madness is terrifying and I was no exception. Were there other mad O'Hagans . . . Uncle Fingal, for instance? But Fiona had told me that the illness was inherited from her mother. I wondered if, despite her denials, she might have a share in that dire bequest but soon discarded this notion as mere wishful thinking.

I was tardy for lunch but it went unnoticed, for the men had returned, David Fallon still among them. As I saw Dimitri in his accustomed place, my heart lifted and my gloomy thoughts dispersed like wind-scattered storm clouds, the while my other self censured me sternly and resolutely restrained the smile my lips would have given him.

As I slipped into my place, he had no difficulty in smiling at me. "Miss Ayers, I was thinking that the children had proved too much for you and you'd hidden yourself away."

"On the contrary," I replied, "I find them charming!" I looked down the table to where they sat and smiled— Kevin, finding my eyes on him, characteristically stuck out his tongue. Forgetting myself, I made a horrible face back at him and, hearing Dimitri's low laugh in my ear, I blushed.

"Admirable, Miss Ayers," he murmured, "you have certainly discovered the proper language with which to communicate."

Embarrassed, I replied, "They're just like my little brothers and sisters." Then, desirous of changing the subject, I added, "Did you enjoy your hunting?"

He looked at me a second before replying, then he said audaciously, "Yes, Miss Ayers, we had good hunting but I'm not sure but that there's better sport closer to home."

For the first time, I discovered just what it meant to have your heart leap, but I said merely, "Is that so?"

"Yes, that is——" he broke off suddenly and I, looking

up, saw Fiona enter. With a pang, I noted that she had changed her gown and looked entrancing in rose-colored silk. With the lightness of a dandelion puff, she floated across the floor.

"Oh," she said, her blue gaze seemingly embracing everyone in the room, "you're all back . . . Cousin David and Dimitri and . . ."

"Uncle Conan and Uncle Patrick," Conan finished derisively.

"Fiona," Lady Kathleen ordered, "why are you so late? Your soup is cold."

"Oh, Aunt Kathleen," she shrugged, "I am not at all hungry. Lucy, didn't you make my excuses for me?"

"I—" I began, flushing, for I had forgotten all about her.

"It's not up to Miss Ayers to make your excuses for you, Fiona," Lady Kathleen said tartly. "You know the hour at which we dine."

I saw David Fallon's eyes rest on his cousin. "Fiona," he said.

"Yes, Cousin David?" she inquired brightly.

He made a convulsive movement and the wineglass before him toppled, staining the cloth scarlet. "What?"

As the footman behind him bent over to mop up the wine and replenish the glass, Fiona said with the suspicion of a giggle, "You spoke my name."

"I did?" he responded blankly, looking bemused.

Laughter circulated around the room and Lord Concullen, sitting next to David, patted him gently on the shoulder. "Come, lad, you've not the time to be mooning over Fiona, you're a man of action."

Dimitri frowned and my heart turned over. I was sure that his jealousy had been aroused. Turning my face away, I met Conan's cool eyes, lit with inner fires of amusement, much of which, I feared, was directed at me. Why I should afford him amusement, I did not know, for I could only guess at the workings of his mind—largely, however, he still remained an enigma to me. For one thing, I could not imagine why he chose to live in the castle. Unlike his cousins, he did not fit neatly into his surroundings. He possessed a cool sophistication which, in my estimation, would have served him better in a large city such as London or Paris. It occurred to me that he added very little in the way of conversation to any gathering in which he appeared, yet I was sure that he had a ready wit—I could see it flickering in his eyes.

"Yes, Miss Ayers?" he said suddenly.

I looked away hastily, for I had been staring at him and he had caught me at it. "I—beg your pardon, sir?" I stammered.

"Come—why do you look away, Miss Ayers," he said softly. "Let me see your eyes—they are quite amazing, you know—like twin pools of sunlight trapped in an amber glass."

I am sure I blushed. His gallantry was both unsettling and embarrassing, but before I could think of an appropriate response, Lady Kathleen shook her finger at him reprovingly.

"Conan, let the child finish her meal in peace." She smiled at me. "Don't pay any attention to my cousin-in-law—he *will* tease!"

Embarrassed, I smiled wanly at her and fastened my attention resolutely on my plate, refusing to look up lest I should meet Conan's mocking eyes again, but I felt them on me and resented him thoroughly, since isolated in my own self-consciousness, I could not join in the conversation. Fiona, utterly undisturbed by any undercurrents, continued to laugh and chatter with David and Dimitri, successfully holding the attention of both.

In the hour that passed between lunch and lessons, I hoped I would be able to escape to my own room but instead, Dimitri proposed a walk—this time he chose to stroll along the sea wall. Both Marra and Kevin gleefully assented and I tried to appear enthusiastic. Fiona, hearing his invitation, disappeared. I knew without asking that she had gone to change her clothes, and sure enough, as I, in lieu of Molly, buttoned the children into their coats and cloaks, she appeared, looking beautiful in a swirling blue cloth cape with a fetching silk-lined hood. Not surprisingly, David Fallon asked if he might join us and I thought I discerned the barest flash of anger in Fiona's eyes, but the next moment, she was gaily tucking her hand in his and pulling him across the hall toward the door.

When we came out to walk by the waist-high brick wall that sheltered our path from the cliff's edge, the beauty of the day heightened my spirits. The air was so fresh and the sky such a vivid blue! The waves shimmered and it seemed to me that the sun had turned the green hills into polished emeralds. Dimitri came to stand beside me.

"You look entranced, Miss Ayers."

"I am—it's so beautiful here."

"Yes," he nodded, "it is sufficiently picturesque, I believe. Perhaps you'll want to set up your easel and sketch it one afternoon."

I shook my head. "I would not do justice to it. It is too lovely to be reproduced in any medium."

"Yes, some beauty has that effect on one—now I am wondering whether they are sunlight or moonshine?"

"Sir?" I exclaimed, startled by the nonsequitur.

"Or—are they twin topazes. No, I'd not call them topaz—because that's a semi-precious stone and sure these are of the first water."

"Oh! Now I understand. You heard Conan teasing me and you're following suit."

"But I'm not teasing you, Miss Ayers," he smiled, "only commenting on a fortunate possession. No, do not lower them—I like to look into them."

Before I could comment further on this outrageous badinage, Fiona exclaimed suddenly, "Marra, Kevin, keep away from the edge! Really, Lucy, you should watch them—not stay way back there with Dimitri!"

Unused to rebukes from Fiona, I felt more angry than guilty, but in the next moment, I was startled by a long wailing cry. I stopped short, transfixed by horror. Had one of the children fallen? With an exclamation, I rushed on ahead to find them both standing motionless on the path, their eyes wide with terror. Kevin had turned so pale that all his freckles stood out like ink dots and Marra, running to me, hid her face in my skirts. Again the cry reverberated in my ears and I became aware of the sea plunging and hissing against the jagged seamed cliffs.

"Has someone fallen in the water, then?"

Marra looked up at me. "That's our Meg," she whimpered.

Again the wail was repeated and this time I fancied I heard, "Doom . . . Doom . . . Doom for the O'Hagans."

Leaving the children, I dashed back and looked toward the spot where the banshee usually stood. Finally, I saw her high on another rock but there was no hint of the elfin mischief that had illumined her face during our conversation. In thrall to her rules, Meg appeared pale and haggard. Her eyes were sunken in dark pits and her red locks, lifted by the wind, writhed around her face like Medusa's snakes. In another second, she had faded from view.

I walked slowly back to the others and we exchanged distraught glances. David, I noted, had paled beneath his tan. In subdued tones, he said to Dimitri, "It was the banshee, then?"

Dimitri nodded, his mouth grim. "Yes, and ill-wishing one of us."

Fiona also nodded. "One of us will not last the night through."

At that, the children began to weep in unison and Dimitri said sharply, "You do not know that for a fact." He knelt down beside the frightened pair and put his arms around them. "Now, now, stop that," he soothed. "That warning was not necessarily directed at one of *us* right here—it might affect any one of the O'Hagans."

"But that's what I meant, dear Dimitri," Fiona replied. "Any one of the O'Hagans. The last time Meg predicted doom, it was a second gardener dropped dead and no one knew he was even a relation!" She rolled her eyes and winked at Kevin and Marra, who were somewhat cheered by her outrageous confidence, though I doubt they understood its full import. However, no one wanted to continue the walk and we were all glad enough to return to the great hall with its roaring fire and its air of indestructibility.

If the children had been reassured by Fiona, I was not so sanguine. As the afternoon wore on, I longed to seek out Meg, but conversly I had no real wish to speak with her. I could not drive the vision of her pallid features from my mind nor could I forget that she had predicted doom—most of all, I prayed that it would not descend upon Dimitri.

My pupils were no more comfortable than I. They were so restless and ill-at-ease that I had decided to excuse them and had just started to issue the order when Lady Kathleen came in.

"Miss Ayers," she said, "I think you may dismiss the children for the rest of the afternoon."

"Oh, I was just about to do so," I said. Then fearing I might have overstepped my authority, I added, "We've all had such difficulty concentrating."

"I quite understand," she said.

"Mama, Mama," Marra cried, "we heard the wicked banshee."

"It screeched three times!" shuddered Kevin.

"I know," Lady Kathleen kissed Marra and tousled Kevin's hair, "and you must not worry now. Why don't you go down to the kitchen? I have it on good authority that cook has baked some chocolate cake."

They needed no further prompting and disappeared quickly from view. Lady Kathleen, who had been smiling tenderly after them, turned to me, her gravity reappearing. "I understand you heard our Meg, too?"

"Yes, I heard her—I also saw her."

"I hope you've the good sense not to fear for yourself . . . though, it would not hurt if you locked your door tonight."

Her duplication of the Princess' warning startled me, "But if I'm not in—danger . . . ?"

"No, no," she said quickly, "but locking a door is always a wise precaution . . . No, you must not think yourself in any peril, Miss Ayers; it is one of the O'Hagans who must do the worrying."

"I do hope it will be a distant relation," I told her, adding hastily, "that is—if it has to be anyone."

She nodded. "It must be some one of us. Meg's warning always presages a death in the family and though it is selfish of me, I do hope that it will not strike—here."

Another disquieting thought occurred to me. "Would—it happen tonight?"

"Yes, tonight." Lady Kathleen's blue eyes filled with tears. "I must get back to my husband. Oh, it's glad I am that he's home again and not out with all those rough fellows at their work in—uh—hunting." To my consternation, she gave me a strange embarrassed look and as she hurried out, I saw that there was a deep flush on her cheeks.

At the time, however, I was too disturbed by the earlier events of the day to ponder overmuch on her confusion. More depressed than ever, I went to my room. Closing my door, I slipped quickly out of my garments and donned my dressing robe, thinking, as I had more than once, that I really hated my heavy dresses. I had intended to rest for an hour or so but found I could not resist looking out of the window to see if Meg were there. She was not in sight but Fiona and David were—standing at the wall looking out to sea. His arm was clasped about her waist and her head rested on his shoulder. As I looked, they turned toward each other and embraced. To my amazement, she clung fiercely to him, pressing her mouth on his—her little hands reaching inside his shirt. He, on his part, seemed shocked by her passion and broke away from her after an instant. Yet, in another second, he had taken her in his arms once more and he was, as some novelists I have read put it, "raining kisses on her upturned throat" the while she was moaning and twisting her body in a manner that reminded me strongly of my cat during those periods when Mama locked her in the cellar. I was heartily shocked by Fiona's actions and felt dimly that it was my duty to report them to her cousin, but then I reflected I had no reason to interfere—she was not one of my charges and besides—as her bosom friend—I could not betray her. As I turned away from the window, I did not scruple to ask myself what I would have done had the man been Dimitri. For the sake of my position and my peace of mind, I was glad that he was not, and immediately, the prospect of dinner did not seem as wearisome as it had before. I even forgot that there was a doom hanging over the inmates of O'Hagan's Keep that night.

As I had anticipated, dinner started out delightfully. The Princess had retired early with a headache and Fiona seemed completely absorbed in David Fallon. I was generous enough to admit to myself that they would make a lovely couple—her beauty and his striking good looks. Regarding them, I felt almost benign, like a matchmaking maiden aunt. Then I forgot about them, for Dimitri was speaking to me. Even though I did not approve the subject matter of our conversation, I found it fascinating to listen to him—mainly because he looked at me with such warmth in his slanted brown eyes. He was telling me about a stag hunt—of the vicious way in which the poor embattled creature used its antlers to gouge the hunting dogs, as why should it not, being just one among many and fighting desperately but futilely for its right to live in the green forest. I do not hold with hunting—nor in any sport that must needs threaten the life of man or beast. Yet, as I listened to Dimitri, I could almost put aside my prejudices and share in the excitement of the chase. I was so totally immersed in what he was telling me that the rest of the conversations around me had assumed the characterless hum of background music, played by a distant ensemble.

"Lucy . . . Lucy . . ." My name spoken softly but insistently caused me to turn from Dimitri to Fiona, who stared at me, a trace of impatience in her manner.

"Yes, Fiona?"

"Tell David how well I am doing in my French conversation, he does not believe it from me but . . ."

"Now, Fiona," David started to protest, "I did not infer . . . !"

"But he will from my *governess,*" she finished triumphantly, having achieved her real purpose, which was to remind me of my place in her world.

Dimitri frowned. "Because Miss Ayers is kind enough to give you a few lessons does not make her your *governess,* Fiona," he observed coldly.

"Well, she's Marra, Kevin, and Brian's governess, isn't she?" demanded Fiona, inadvertently betraying her true intentions.

"Fiona!" Lady Kathleen exclaimed, "you are being rude to Miss Ayers. Ask her pardon at once!"

"Am I being rude, dear Lucy?" Fiona's eyes, wide and guileless, met mine. "Of a truth, I did not mean it so."

In spite of my inward anger, I smiled easily back at her. "I was not aware of any rudeness, Fiona," I returned calmly, "and yes indeed, Mr. Fallon, she speaks an excellent French. She's had able instruction in the language, though I myself cannot take credit for it—that must go to my predecessor, I imagine."

"Very neatly put, Miss Ayers," approved Conan.

I looked at him blankly, not knowing whether or not I should acknowledge his compliment and then I stiffened, actually impaled by the expression in his gray eyes—it seemed to strip the garb from my body and linger lasciviously on my bare flesh. I had never before suspected him of even a passing interest in women—or more specifically me—and yet, at that moment, I felt threatened by a lust so obvious that it was almost palpable. In another second, his heavy lids dropped down over his eyes and then, only then could I turn away. Conscious that I was breathing rather quickly, I tried to quell my nervousness and I fixed my attention on Dimitri again. Yet, though we resumed our conversation, our rapport had fled—he was preoccupied, reminded probably of Fiona's existence, which was another goal she had hoped to achieve, no doubt. I myself, relegated to the place of an upper servant, was feeling hurt and quite angry with Miss Charlotte Brontë for having created a fiction that had changed the course of my life. If it had not been for *Jane Eyre,* I am quite sure I should have been able to persuade Mama to send Imogen in my place, while who knows—I might have followed Oriana to London, since she had written asking me to come there on a visit.

After dinner, we went into the music room, but there was no singing that night. Fiona excused herself early, pleading a headache, and David, too, went early to bed, telling us that he was bone-weary.

Conan moved restively around the room and stopping at a window pulled aside a drape, commenting, "Look, the moon has risen."

"Has it?" Lady Kathleen spoke breathlessly, and following Conan, she stood beside him, staring out the window. Her husband arose from his chair and walked leisurely across the room to stand behind her, putting his big hand on her shoulder in a gesture that seemed half caress, half support. Though she was generally completely in command of herself, I saw her lean gratefully against him, the while she still stared at the moon, hanging like a huge silver pendant on the bosom of the sky.

Remembering what Fiona had told me about Brian's infirmity, I shuddered. I wondered what form his madness took and could only be thankful for the oaken door that stood between him and the castle corridors. However, since I did not want to betray a knowledge I had no right to possess, I joined them all at the window and said, "Oh, it's a full moon. How beautiful it looks!"

"Your rising moon that looks for us again . . ." Conan quoted softly and turning from the window, looked at me. "Do you know that stanza, Miss Ayers? Can you repeat the rest of it?"

I nodded. "How oft, hereafter will she wax and wane . . . how oft, hereafter, rising look for us through this same garden, and for *one* in vain."

"Oh," Lady Kathleen turned away from the window, shivering, "that's a melancholy bit of verse."

Conan laughed. "Naturally it's melancholy—a crabbed English-Irishman, if we go by the name, interpreting the sentiments of a Persian tentmaker."

"Omar Khayyám," Dimitri identified, "translated by Edward Fitzgerald. It was published only six or seven years ago. How did you happen on it, Miss Ayers?"

"My teacher gave it to me," I answered, a vivid picture of Miss Vyvyan coming to my mind, spots of color in her pale cheeks and her cultured voice lingering caressingly over each syllable as she quoted

> "The Worldly Hope men set their Hearts upon,
> Turns Ashes—or it prospers; and anon
> Like snow upon the Desert's dusty Face,
> Lighting a little hour or two, was gone."

"Oh, Lucy!" she had brought her thin hands together soundlessly, "How true . . . how sadly true . . ."

Conan flung another round of verses at me, interrupting my thoughts . . .

> "There was the Door to which I found no Key;
> There was the Veil through which I might not see:
> Some little talk awhile of Me and Thee
> There was—and then no more of Thee and Me."

> "Ah, make the most of what we may yet spend,
> Before we, too, into the dust descend,
> Dust into Dust and under Dust to lie,
> Sans Wine, sans Song, sans Singer and sans End."

He held his hand up curved as if around a cup. "I approve of your education," he told me.

Lady Kathleen shook her head. "Come—no more of this Persian, Conan, please."

He laughed at her. "Blame Miss Ayers, it's she who raised his spirit from the dead. Miss Ayers who communes with banshees and the like."

Lady Kathleen winced and drew closer to Lord Concullen, who put his arm around her. "Stop talking about banshees, Conan!" he ordered.

Conan shrugged. "Sorry, Kathie," he told her, kissing her on the cheek and adding, " 'O my dark Rosaleen, Do not sigh do not weep' . . . though you are a light Rosaleen, dear Kathie." He looked at me, his gray eyes alight with malicious humor. "I'm off to bed to dream of Persians with golden eyes." Bowing slightly he left the room.

"Now you're not to pay any attention to him, Miss

Ayers," Lady Kathleen exclaimed as he went. "It's a perverse spirit that seizes him at times."

"And he has a twisted tongue at all times," growled Dimitri.

"Oh," I shrugged, "I'm sure he means nothing at all by it." Inwardly, I was not so sure. Conan's teasing had had an odd effect on me. Certain parts of my—anatomy throbbed and burned. I could not imagine why and I found the sensation both embarrassing and provoking.

"What time is it?" Lady Kathleen demanded suddenly.

"There's the clock." Lord Concullen pointed to the domed French timepiece on the mantel. Its gilded hands indicated the hour of eight thirty.

"It will be a long night," Lady Kathleen said. "I wish there was a way of rushing it."

Lord Concullen laughed and, moving from her, he walked to the pianoforte. "Come, love, I'll play you a jig." He made good his threat but though he performed well enough, the music sounded discordant.

"It's out of tune," groaned Dimitri, his hands to his ears. "Stop it, Pat."

"It wasn't out of tune last night," Lady Kathleen said.

"It's the moon that's affected its keys," Dimitri responded, "its keys and Conan's tongue and the lot of us. We'd best retire for the night and sleep."

It was a suggestion I welcomed. Gratefully, I arose and bid them good night, hoping I would see them all in the morning. The *all,* of course, translated into Dimitri.

Yet, the minute I left that well-lighted room for the shadowy halls, I wished I had not been so quick to go. My fears of the morning, supported by the events of the day, had increased and, as I hurried to my room, it seemed to me that the air was heavy with menace. Furthermore, as I ascended the stairs leading to the corridor where my chamber was located, I heard a faint sound behind me—a panting and a whimpering not unlike that which had issued from back of Brian's door. Remembering the chain, I told myself it was my imagination, but still I hastened my footsteps—in fact, I ran, and, opening my door, I slipped inside, shutting and locking it. I leaned against it for a moment, trembling like the proverbial aspen leaf. As I stood there, striving to regain my equilibrium, a loud noise shattered the stillness. I screamed in terror and then felt remarkably foolish, for in another second I had traced the sound to my window which had been blown open by a gust of wind. Thankfully, I went to close it and, as I did, saw that the full moon had flung a broad carpet of shifting light across the inky waters to the shore-line where it was fragmented against the swirling spray. For a moment, I remained at my window enthralled by that chill and solemn beauty, then I heard the flapping of giant wings and looking up, I saw outlined against the moon an immense bat. Wheeling and squeaking it disappeared into the darkness, effectively shattering my brief communion with nature. I do not like bats. I remembered with a shudder being told that if one gets tangled in your hair, it has to be cut out. Hastily, I closed the window and prepared for bed, thinking dismally that I would probably not sleep at all. However, despite my fears, I fell immediately into a deep slumber.

Hours later, I awakened with a start. I had been dreaming of a puppy and, upon awakening, I still heard its growls and snufflings. In fact, it seemed to be right outside my door. I lay listening for a second, wondering if I was still dreaming. Pinching my arm, I discovered that I was not and, aware that I still heard beseeching puppy paws scratching at my door, I sat up, nodding my head sagely. Despite Molly's vehement denials, there had been a dog in Brian's room that morning—brought in, possibly, to pacify the poor child. Perhaps it had become frightened and run from him. At that moment, I became drowsily indignant with Molly for even hinting that the noises I had heard might have been made by Brian—it was definitely a dog. Though I was still half-asleep, I slid from my bed and ran across the chilly floor to let it in, but as I started to turn the key, I heard a snarling yap and froze, remembering belatedly that Mama had always warned us about being too friendly to strange dogs. The animal outside might be vicious, especially if it had been closeted with a demented little boy. Though I longed to cuddle it, I decided it was best to resist this temptation and, reluctantly, I went back to bed, resolutely closing my ears to the whimperings of my canine visitor. It scratched on my door for several minutes more, but I ignored it and finally managed to go to sleep again.

I awakened to bright sunshine, blue skies, and a subdued ocean, serenely lapping at the rocks below. It was a lovely morning and one that helped me to vanquish the fears of the night. I did not even wait for the arrival of Agnes and my tea. I hurried through my dressing and was plaiting my hair when all of a sudden I heard a crash of china outside my door. I unlocked it to find Agnes staring blankly at her fallen tray.

"Oh, Miss," she sobbed, "I'm ever so sorry."

"Come, Agnes, don't cry," I said bracingly. "Accidents do happen. I'll get a towel to mop up the tea and you come on inside and sit down."

"Oh, miss," she sniffed, "it—it was the door that made me do it."

"The door?" I repeated.

"L-Look at it, m-miss." She pointed a shaking finger at it. "Those—those marks wasn't there yesterday."

Staring at it, I saw that its dark surface was indeed considerably marred by deep scratches.

"My, he did make a mess of it, didn't he!"

"He? Who?" she exclaimed fearfully.

"The dog."

"Dog! What dog? There's not one of 'em in the whole castle."

I explained the noises I had heard outside my door the previous night and, to my surprise, she turned alarmingly pale. "A puppy," she repeated, "and you did not let it in because you were—were not—sure it was friendly?"

"That is correct, Agnes," I answered, wondering not a little at her reaction. "Mama always cautioned us to beware of strange dogs."

At that Agnes laughed loudly in a manner I can only describe as hysterical. When she had calmed down, she gasped, "It's thankful you should be to your mama, miss, and I hope you'll be remembering her in your prayers, this night and every night to come."

"Of course, I shall, I always do," I said virtuously if erroneously. "But, Agnes, what is the matter with you? What is that gesture you're making?"

"It's the sign of the cross, miss."

"Why?"

"I just had to cross myself, miss. It's comforting some-how . . . If—if you'll excuse me, I—I'll be fetching you another cup of tea." Before I could protest that I did not want any tea, she had scuttled down the hall.

I did not wait for her to return. I went down to breakfast. As I traversed those gloomy halls, I suddenly remembered Meg's predictions and felt that familiar pounding in my throat, but Agnes, I recalled, had said nothing about any death in the castle. Though that cheered me a little, I still hastened my footsteps, but when I reached the breakfast room, I found most of the family assembled—only Fiona and David were not present. As I came in, I noticed various curious looks directed at me, from which I guessed that Agnes had not been silent about my midnight disturbance. A second later, I knew she had not, for Lady Kathleen surged forward. "My dear Miss Ayers," she said anxiously, "I understand that you had a—a rather bad fright last night."

"I wasn't frightened, Lady Kathleen," I replied. "In fact, I fell asleep immediately afterward."

"Ah, youth, youth," murmured the Princess.

"I'm glad," Lady Kathleen said, "that you had the good sense not to open your door."

"Oh, well," I shrugged, "I don't suppose I'd have taken much harm from it. It sounded like quite a young puppy."

A choking sound came from Dimitri, who, as his mother patted him solicitously on the back, explained that he had swallowed a piece of toast the wrong way.

"You must always be wary of strange dogs," Conan told me, putting his hand lightly on mine.

Again, I experienced that strange sensation and, finding it not to my liking, I moved away from him. "My mama told me the same thing."

"Your mother is an intelligent woman," Lord Concullen said.

Tiring of their innuendo, I asked the obvious question. "If it wasn't a dog, what was it?"

There was a surprised silence and then Dimitri said slowly, "There are other animals in this vicinity, Miss Ayers—other wilder animals. We do not know what scratched at your door last night, but all of us are glad you did not open it. It might have been a strange dog, though, as you have been told, there are none in the castle—or it might have been something more dangerous."

"But—what!?" I demanded. "And if it were another animal, how could it have gotten into the castle?"

"There are ways, Miss Ayers," the Princess said, suddenly pressing her hand to her forehead. "Yes, there are ways that you cannot imagine."

"Maman," Dimitri put his arms around her. "Try not to think about it now, please."

With a slight shock I remembered that it had been she who had urged me to lock my door. What had she feared?

"Tanya," Lady Kathleen went to her, "it was an accident. Molly . . ."

"Kathleen!" Lord Concullen frowned at her.

"I suggest that you take the Princess to her room, Dimitri," Conan said. "Obviously, she is distraught and . . ."

At that moment, there was a furious pounding on the garden door and, through the window, I could see the agitated face of an under-gardener. Dimitri hastily admitted him.

"Well, Rory, what seems to be the matter?"

"Oh, sir—you—you've got to come outside," gasped the man.

"Rory, what is it!" Lord Concullen strode to his side.

"It—it's Mr. Fallon—and—and—" To my consternation, he burst into tears.

"Where is he?" Dimitri spoke through stiff lips. "Come —take us to him."

Still sobbing, the gardener turned and went out, Dimitri, Lord Concullen, and Conan following him, while Lady Kathleen stood stricken, a hand to her heart.

"Oh," she cried, "I—have a premonition."

"No, please God, no." The Princess, who had become very pale, sat hastily down on a chair as if her legs had suddenly ceased to function. Reaching into a pocket in her dress, she produced a small string of bright beads with a golden cross dangling from them and began to pass them agitatedly through her fingers, murmuring inarticulately as she did so.

I stood where I was, not knowing what to do but feeling that I had to find out what had happened to David Fallon. In a few moments, Dimitri and Lord Concullen returned, looking pale and grim. The Princess raised her eyes and looked at her son. In a cold little voice, she said, "It has happened again?"

"Has it?" cried Lady Kathleen.

Dimitri looked at the two women. "Maman," he said gently, "you'd best go to your room."

"It has happened again," said the Princess, still in that frozen whisper.

Dimitri nodded, then, as if he had expected it, he rushed to his mother's chair in time to catch her limp body in his arms and bear her from the room.

Lady Kathleen, pale as the little white ruffles bordering her collar, asked, "It—it was the same as Sean?"

"So—it appears," Lord Concullen nodded.

"But how . . ." she shook her head and fell silent.

I could bear the suspense no longer. "Tell me what happened to David Fallon!?" I cried.

"He's dead," Lord Concullen said shortly. "Dead in the forest with his throat torn out."

I clutched a chair, for the room had seemed to whirl about me. "Oh, no, no, no," I heard myself repeating.

"Patrick, you shouldn't have told her!" Lady Kathleen exclaimed.

"She'd have heard it from the servants soon enough."

"But—how—how could it have happened? What could have killed him . . . ? A—A wild beast?" Even as I spoke, I remembered the scratches on my door. "What was it—what was abroad last night?"

It was Conan, who answered me—Conan, who must have heard my semihysterical questions as he came in from the garden.

"Let us call it a wolf, Miss Ayers," he said.

"A wolf!?" I stared at him incredulously. "But . . ."

"As you have been told, Miss Ayers, there are wolves in Ireland."

"Wolves that lurk in the castle halls?!" I cried. "Wolves that hunt in the garden?"

"In the garden?" Conan questioned. "What do you know about that?"

"Fiona . . ." I began, and then I thought about Fiona and David as I had seen them by the sea wall yesterday afternoon. "Oh, poor Fiona!" I gasped.

"Why poor Fiona?" Conan asked me dryly.

I resented an enmity that could express itself even at this tragic moment. "She—seemed to—like her Cousin David so much," I said.

"That's true," moaned Lady Kathleen, "and someone will have to tell her. Where is she? I've not seen her this morning?"

"Oh, God," I cried, "where is she, indeed?"

Lady Kathleen turned on me, her blue eyes blazing. "Miss Ayers, what would you be hinting?" she demanded.

"I—I've seen them—to—together so often," I faltered, wondering what I had said to arouse her, "I—only feared that—that she might have—been with him—last night . . ."

"No!" Lord Concullen exclaimed in horrified accents, "not little Fiona. She has none of—of——"

"Patrick!" Conan spoke sharply, "Miss Ayers is worried about Fiona's safety." He turned on me. "That's the way of it, isn't it?"

"Why yes," I said, at a loss to understand their expressions of shock and repugnance.

"I think," Conan said, "you'll find her safely asleep in her bed, but if you have any doubts, I suggest you go and see for yourselves."

We went, all of us—terrified, except for Conan, whose calm remained unbroken. As he had prophesied, we found her sleeping and in pity did not waken her, for, as Lady Kathleen said, she would find out soon enough.


In the next two days, the castle was filled with strangers—grim men from the village, who consulted with Lord Concullen, Dimitri, and Conan. For some reason, Uncle Fingal remained aloof and did not make an appearance at these meetings.

On the morning of the second day after David Fallon's death, an inquest was held which, fortunately, I was not required to attend. I spent those hours reading to my depressed and inattentive pupils. At noon, we learned that the verdict had been death by misadventure—the culprit was believed to be a renegade wolf or maddened dog. I learned from Agnes, however, that the more fanciful of the villagers muttered darkly about ancient curses and supernatural intervention, whispering tales of giant predatory birds hatched from dragons' eggs, about pookas, witches, and even the fairy folk.

In the castle, the servants were restive and unhappy. Again, through Agnes, I heard that Mary, the cook, wanted to leave but loyalty to Lady Kathleen kept her trembling at her stove, though she would hang garlands of smelly seaweed in the larder to ward off the evil spirits, a superstition she had inherited from her Welsh grandmother. Nonnie, the kitchen maid, did leave and in her place was the untrained but also unterrified Bridie, who found the castle pantries to her liking and none to chide her for the snatching of a cake or pasty, maids being difficult to find. John and Timothy, the two footmen, and Riordan, the butler, were young enough to be excited rather than alarmed by the tragedy and bored below-stairs gatherings with their endless speculations of the species of beast that had killed David Fallon. Danny O'Toole, the foxy-faced handyman who had brought me from the station, subscribed to the wolf-theory, but Rory, the second gardener, and Dermot, his superior, had an entirely different idea—one Agnes confided to me with many apologies—they blamed the English.

"The English?" I had questioned when she told me, "but there are none around here except me. They can't think that I . . ."

"Not you, miss," she hastily answered, "but there are English in the neighborhood—a whole garrison of the bas—of them—stationed beyond the village in Conn's Castle, which they appropriated after the owner died. It's after the boys, they are—the bloody vultures!"

"The boys," I had mused, thinking of my conversation with Mrs. Costello. "Not the I.R.B.?"

Agnes had stared at me, her eyes filled with dismay. "And what would you be knowing about them, miss?" she had whispered.

"Nothing, but Agnes . . ."

"Excuse me, miss, I hear my bell," she had told me firmly and rushed away in answer to this spurious summons. I had wondered then and still wondered if David Fallon had had any connection with the I.R.B. I did not find it difficult to believe, nor would I have been surprised if others in that household knew far more about that organization than might be expected of "wealthy landowners." It would have explained their secretive looks and also that hunting expedition about which the women had been so perturbed. It did not, however, explain to me my alien presence in O'Hagan's Keep.

The day following the inquest, David Fallon's funeral took place. The service was conducted by a priest from the village, who stood at the pulpit in the ancient chapel adjoining the family plot. Aside from the O'Hagans, several young men from the surrounding area attended and, after the mass, I saw several of them gather around Lord Concullen and Dimitri. Purposefully passing close to them, I heard one of them say, "Who's to do it now?" I heard Dimitri reply, "Never fear, it will be done."

In that moment, someone caught sight of me and I received a suspicious glare from the strangers before they turned and went outside, accompanied by Lord Concullen and Dimitri. A second later, Conan too arose and started after them. As he passed me, he looked full at me and I saw the tip of his tongue emerge from his mouth and travel slowly over his lips, an action that revolted me, though I knew not why. I averted my head hastily and sank down in a pew, shuddering.

In another second, however, I had forgotten my own distress, for I heard the sound of sobbing and, turning, I found Fiona kneeling beside me, her head bowed on the carved seat in front of her. It occurred to me that I had seen very little of her in the last three days and, when she raised her head, I was shocked at the change in her. Pallid and wan, there were dark circles under her eyes and her cheeks seemed sunken. She was clad in the deepest mourning.

"Fiona," I said gently, "dear Fiona, I am sorry. I wish there was something I could do for you."

Sob after sob shook her. "No one can help me, no one. I am lost . . . lost."

I put my arm around her but to my surprise, she shrank away. "You must not touch me," she whispered, "no one must touch me."

Rather hurt, I moved back and then with a loud wail, Fiona suddenly hurled herself forward, burying her face on my lap. "Oh, Lucy, Lucy, Lucy, what am I to do?"

"Poor Fiona," I touched her bowed golden head with its dark veil half pulled away. "Did he mean so much to you, then, David?"

Her face still muffled in my skirts, she sobbed, "Oh, God, I wish that I might lie in the grave with him and be peaceful, at last!"

Agonized as those words were, their sentiment seemed too extravagant to me—as if, instead of suffering real grief, she were reveling in its facsimile. My concern turned to impatience and I moved restively under her clutching hands. "Fiona," I said crisply, "you are far too young to speak in such a manner and furthermore, your attachment to your cousin was certainly not of a long duration."

She raised her face, then, tears still pouring from her eyes. "Lucy, Lucy, you do not understand. You—do not know how—he died."

"How—he died?" I echoed.

Nodding, she clutched my hand. "I—I was to—to meet him in the—woods. I—arrived too late—and saw—" she shuddered and swallowed painfully, "I saw him dead and—and I know what killed him."

"You—know!!!" I cried.

"Hush!" she whispered, looking around us, but there was no one left in the chapel.

"But—if you know—why have you told no one?" I asked.

"Because—because of my—brother—Brian."

"Brian?" I echoed.

"Lucy, it was Brian who killed David, I am sure of it."

For a second I was struck dumb. I could only stare at her, wondering if I were going out of my mind, for certainly I had not heard aright. "Brian?" I gasped finally. "But—how could he . . ."

"It was Molly, that fool, who fell asleep and—and somehow—he slipped his chain and got away. He's more than cunning when the madness is upon him—and he's very strong, too." Another fit of sobbing shook her. "What do you think scratched at your door the other night, Lucy? That was Brian! Brian—out for blood."

"B-Brian—but it sounded like a—"

"I know—that's part of it—and you—you were protected—protected by—by some heavenly power—for if—if you had opened your door, Lucy—oh, my dear Lucy." She held my hand against her wet cheek. "But you did not—and he—he must have run into the forest and—he —he found David."

"But David's throat was . . ."

"Yes, I know . . . I saw it—torn and . . . but Lucy, Brian—did not mean to kill David—it—it is any thing— any person he sees when the moon is high—he cannot help himself! And—and if I told, they'd hunt him down, poor Brian, and shoot him with a—a silver bullet—a consecrated bullet—as—as they did poor Mama."

"The hunting accident . . . *that* was the hunting accident?" I gasped.

"Yes, yes, yes!" she wept.

"But you said—the Princess . . ."

"I lied—no, it was not a lie—I couldn't tell you the whole truth then, Lucy, but hear—it now . . . It was the Princess who betrayed her. Dimitri's father loved my mother and it was for her he went to Russia to search for a drug that might cure—her. He found nothing and unable to—save her, he—tried to love another and so married the Princess and told her my mother's secret! When—when they came home—he found he still loved my mother—and could not—live without her. The Princess—in revenge . . ." Again, she began to cry, heartbrokenly.

Shocking as her story was, I must admit that I was considerably more horrified by my own narrow escape from the fate that had overtaken David Fallon. Furthermore, I found myself extremely angry with the O'Hagans—Dimitri, included—for certainly they should not have hired me to instruct a werewolf.

Too, I wondered why I had not suspected as much. I had done enough reading in the occult to be quite familiar with the legend and now that I thought of it, there had been several indications of the true state of affairs. That I had failed to interpret them was, I decided, pure chauvinism. As a British subject, I was unwilling to believe that such a beast might lurk in any of our Isles—even Ireland. In common with the rest of my countrymen, I preferred to believe these animals indigenous to France, Germany, and other primitive countries.

As I sat there, unable to put my chaotic thoughts into words, Fiona fastened her hand on my wrist compellingly. "Lucy, I beg you not—not to betray us—Brian and me."

I reminded her that all her other confidences had been safe with me.

"Yes, I—I know, but this time I want you to swear you'll not breathe a word of this—I want you to—to swear it on your immortal soul."

"But, Fiona," I could not help saying, "your family ought to know . . ."

She fell on her knees and clasped her hands. "Lucy, swear—please—please do."

I could not refuse her. Reluctantly, I answered, "Oh, very well—I swear."

"On your immortal soul!" she begged.

With a sigh, I echoed, "On my immortal soul."


After the coffin had been lowered into the grave, Fiona disappeared. I, too, craved solitude, but I still had the children in my care—both of them sadly dispirited, and though I did my best to cheer them, I could do little to alleviate their gloom since I was still preoccupied with Fiona's shocking revelation. I took them to the schoolroom and read them fairy stories but I am afraid I did so with little zest—nor could I bring myself to look at them, for every time I raised my eyes from my book, I imagined that I saw Brian sitting in his accustomed seat, staring at me with those innocent blue eyes, Brian who had torn out his cousin's throat! And would they—when he was well again—bring him downstairs as if nothing had happened?

"Kevin," I could not resist the question, "how is Brian this afternoon?"

Kevin exchanged a glance with Marra and I found myself wondering if they, too, were aware of the secret. I doubted it. "Brian's still sick," Kevin said.

"Danny is tending him," Marra added.

"But where's Molly?"

They shrugged. "Molly's sick, too," Kevin said.

"But I thought Brian did not have a contagious disease," I prodded, thinking to myself that Molly must have been dismissed for her carelessness.

"Oh, she's not that kind of sick," Marra answered. "She fell down and bumped her head."

"Bumped her head!" I repeated sharply. "Was she hurt badly?"

"We don't know for sure," Marra said, "but her brother had to carry her when he came for her."

"Her brother took her away?"

"Yesterday afternoon," Kevin nodded. "He said a lot of bad words."

"What sort of words?"

"Mama says that we should not repeat them," Kevin rolled his eyes, "but one of them was bloody and one of them was . . ."

"Kevin Patrick O'Hagan, I'm going to tell Mama on you!" shrilled Marra.

"You hush!" he snarled.

*112*

"I will not!"

"You will, too, or——"

"Miss Ayers, make Kevin stop pulling my hair!"

To have attempted to find out more about Molly's mishap would have been futile; I should have only roused their suspicions, so I said repressively, "Children, let me finish this story." I rattled the pages of the book. I was reading them a tale from the *Arabian Nights* but I was sorely tempted to substitute *Little Red Riding Hood*.

Around four in the afternoon, Lady Kathleen again dismissed my classes. "Poor Miss Ayers," she sighed, "you have fallen into a strange household, have you not? I do want to thank you for your patience and your kindness to my children. We will try and make it up to you, somehow."

Swallowing the questions I longed to ask, I replied, "I am very fond of Marra and Kevin—and uh—Brian, Lady Kathleen."

"And they are fond of you. It's fortunate we are to have you with us. I hope you'll want to stay."

"Oh, yes," I said, not really thinking about what I was saying.

"Good." She pressed my hand and left me.

It was then that I asked myself why I had been so quick to acquiesce. Did I really want to remain in this castle? Did I really want to mingle with disembodied spirits, banshees, and werewolves? And what of the dreadful fate that had overtaken David Fallon? Could I dismiss it so easily from my mind? Could I forget my own peril—the ominous significance of my scratched door? Suddenly, I longed to be out of the castle—away from its shadowy halls and forbidding eyries. I ran down the stairs and out into the garden, going I knew not whither until I heard a low murmur of men's voices, and, looking around me, saw that I was close to that vine-covered Gothic temple. In it, I discerned several burly shapes and thought I also recognized Dimitri. Quickly, I slipped behind a tree and listened, for here was my chance to learn if they did actually belong to the mysterious I.R.B. However, from where I was standing, I could hear nothing. Quietly, I crept out and, approaching the structure, I crouched down between two fallen pillars. They were speaking in very low tones, but in those quiet gardens, I could hear them.

"The bridge," one said, and I recognized Lord Concullen's voice.

"It was to be tonight," said another, "and it's countin' on us they are—the lads."

"I don't know what we'll do without Mr. David . . ." sighed a third man.

"David's not the only one who can pull off the job, Tom." It was Dimitri who spoke.

"But he's trained in the use of those infernal . . ."

"I can handle them, too," Dimitri interrupted.

"As can I," said Lord Concullen.

"Not you, Pat," Dimitri told him quickly. "There's Kathie and the children."

"If it were only Satan's work, I'd be your man!" Those incomprehensible words were uttered by Uncle Fingal.

"Satan's work!" echoed the man they addressed as Tom, indignantly. "It is for God, St. Patrick, and Holy Ireland!"

There was a gasp and a long indrawn hiss of pain. "Please—you know my infirmity!" protested Uncle Fingal. He sighed, "It's times like these that I wish my own blood yet pounded in my veins."

At that moment, I realized what Uncle Fingal was. I must say I was rather surprised.

"Poor Mr. Fingal," said a man I now recognized as Rory. "It's a hard, hard thing to be situated as you are, I should think."

"There's some as has it harder," muttered Tom, "a stake through the heart and buried at the crossroads."

"If you are going to insult me . . ." Uncle Fingal's deep voice throbbed with self-pity.

"No, Tom, that's no way to address Fingal O'Hagan, who did long ago prove himself for Irish freedom—living or dead," declaimed Rory in ringing tones.

"That is enough," Dimitri rasped. "We're not here to discuss Uncle Fingal's patriotism. It's up to us to see that the bridge is destroyed and the ammunition captured from Conn's Castle. Now—will there be men stationed at the fort to attend to its sacking—when we've attacked the bridge?"

"Aye, it's been arranged."

So intent was I on this conversation that at first I was unaware of a chill touch on my hand, but then something squeezed my wrist and looking down I found it encircled by what appeared to be a thick green vine with tiny tendrils. As I started to shake my wrist free, the vine suddenly wriggled and stuck out a long black tongue. My shriek rang out in the stillness, startling both the inmates of the temple and the small green thing, which slipped quickly under the pillar. At that moment, I wished that I might have joined it. Rising hastily, I would have run away but I succeeded only in falling over the pillar. I was helped to my feet roughly by Rory and his companion, Tom, who proved to be very tall and very burly. Behind them were Uncle Fingal, Conan, Lord Concullen, and Dimitri.

"It—it was a snake," I said weakly.

"There are no snakes in Ireland!" snapped Lord Concullen, glaring at me. "What are you doing here?"

"Spying, the damned limey!" growled Rory.

"If it wasn't a snake, it was a lizard," I said. "A green one, though I didn't see that it had limbs. If there are wolves in Ireland, perhaps there are snakes, too."

"We are not interested in your biological conclusions, Miss Ayers," Lord Concullen said crisply. "What were you doing behind the pillar?"

"I—I wasn't behind anything, I—I was just going for a walk and this lizard . . . or snake . . ."

"Liar!" shouted Rory. "You're in the pay of the British!"

"It was a mad plan to hire an Englishwoman, Patrick, I told you so at the time. I told you—you'd but trick yourselves!" intoned Uncle Fingal.

"Trick!" My suspicions had been justified! Too angry to be diplomatic, I accused, "You engaged me so you'd not be suspected of anti-British sentiments—or activities!"

"Ah, she's a clever one—and well paid for it, I've no doubt," Tom said.

"Nonsense, Tom," exclaimed Dimitri, "she's no spy. I do not believe it for an instant." He came to stand at my side, actually grinning at me. "Like all women, she's got a strong vein of curiosity in her makeup—now that's the way of it, isn't it, Lucy?"

It was the first time he had used my given name but the familiarity gave me no pleasure. "That's the truth," I told him bitterly, "but I suppose it won't save my life. How will I die . . . will I be savaged by the werewolf or drained by the vampire." I let my eyes rest meaningfully upon Uncle Fingal.

"Werewolf!" chorused Tom and Rory.

"Yes," I cried triumphantly, forgetting my promise in my extremity. "It was Brian who killed David Fallon!"

"Brian!?" Conan laughed loudly.

Rory, however, looked very grim. "Is that the truth of it, Patrick O'Hagan?"

"Is it?" demanded Tom.

"I'd forgotten they sheltered yet another of the miserable animals," said Rory, "and it's no laughing matter, Mr. Conan."

Conan continued to laugh. "It was not Brian who did it," he said, "he's but seven years old and he's not grown his full set of fangs yet."

"That's the truth," Lord Concullen insisted. "Little Brian could not tear a man's throat out!"

"Then what killed David Fallon?" I cried.

"It was a wild beast from the woods!" Dimitri said.

"Brian was locked in his room most of the night!" Lord Concullen added.

"Then what scratched at my door?" I demanded.

"And what was it hit Molly on the head and she in a coma ever since?" inquired Rory.

"Ah, then, he was out an' runnin'," cried Tom, "an' lustin' for the blood of an Irish patriot!"

"Not out of the castle," Lord Concullen said firmly. "We found him in the hall and took him back to his room. He'd not been on the grounds—there was no dirt on his paws—uh feet."

"And if you kept him so careful, how come he was runnin' through the halls at all?" asked Rory.

"It seems we underestimated his strength," Patrick said soberly. "Heretofore, Molly has always been able to cope with him but this time . . ."

"Somethin' killed David Fallon an' I'm not so sure it was a beast from the woods." To my horror, his eyes rested on me.

"You—you're mad!" I cried.

"Am I, though?" Rory asked.

"Rory, there's no harm in her!" protested Dimitri.

"I wouldn't be too sure of that," Conan said.

I stared at him, horrified. "You can't believe that I—I—"

"She's an Englishwoman and they're all cut from the same cloth," Tom put in.

"No, the idea is nonsense," said Lord Concullen.

116

"Is it?" Uncle Fingal glowered at me. "There's harm in all the English. Wasn't I driven to making a pact with Himself to rid the land of them and wasn't it all futile in the end?"

"Blame that on Himself and yourself and not the English, Uncle Fingal!" flashed Dimitri.

"Sure an' he's witched again!" groaned Rory.

"Aye," Tom agreed, "if Satan was a woman and wore a petticoat, he'd be chasin' it."

"And who is to say that Satan is not a woman?" There was a sinister red gleam in Uncle Fingal's eyes.

To spite him, I crossed myself, but it only drew a gasp of horror from Rory and Tom.

"Did you see that?" Tom whispered. "She did it backwards."

"Backwards, indeed. She's from hell itself." Rory pointed a trembling finger at the ground.

"Possibly," mused Conan, "that might explain everything."

"I am not from hell," I said, stamping my foot. "I am from Devonshire and my father is in Holy Orders!"

"A damned Orangewoman!" howled Rory, seizing my arm roughly.

"A witch in league with Satan!" yelled Tom.

"Yes," drawled Conan, laying a caressing hand on my shoulder, "a pretty little witch."

As I twisted away from him, Dimitri ordered, "Take your hands off her, Conan." He faced them. "All of this is nonsense. She's no spy. Use your common sense."

"Use yours, Dimitri!" counseled Conan. I wished that I might strike him across his odious mocking face. I think it was he who really frightened me the most because I knew instinctively that he did not consider me a spy. Why, then, had he aligned himself on the side of my enemies? What could be his ulterior motive?

Again, I tried to reason with them. "I am not a spy. I am not in the least interested in Anglo-Irish relations. I know nothing about politics!"

Dimitri and Patrick both argued for me but they were outnumbered. Rory and Tom, with the support of Uncle Fingal and Conan, determined that I must not be released until the night's work had been accomplished.

It was at their insistence that I was led through the woods to a small dark cottage that smelled strongly of

*117*

goats. There I was pushed down on a rough chair, to which they bound me, and then they left me with a gag in my mouth and terror in my heart.

As they went out, I heard Dimitri say hotly, "It's a damned shame, Conan. I don't believe she cares tuppence for the Cause, one way or the other!"

His championship, though singularly ineffective, would have pleased me greatly had I not, as I thought, had my eyes opened to the deficiencies in his character. I had no doubt that if I, in common with my predecessors, disappeared, the next governess would soon be the recipient of his flattering attentions. Practically speaking, there was little in the way of feminine society from which to choose at O'Hagan's Keep. Fervently, I prayed that the next governess would be knock-kneed, squint-eyed, and at least thirty years old.

During the next half hour or so, I struggled in vain to free myself but only succeeded in making myself more uncomfortable. Finally, I sank into a semistupor and I do not know how long I sat there. I only know that it was my own sneezing that roused me. I had sneezed about four times before I realized that there was a most peculiar smell in the room—rather like rotten eggs. I tried to control myself, for it is very difficult to sneeze with a gag in your mouth—in fact, I nearly choked. Then, suddenly, I heard a low laugh and looking up saw a tall man in green, grinning at me. He stood with his back to the door as if he had just entered, but certainly he had moved softly, for I had not heard the creak of the rusty hinge nor, when I came to think of it, had I felt the usual gust of air driven in on my face. As I looked up at him, the smell grew even stronger. I sneezed again.

"Well, well, well," he said. "And what might you be doing here?"

Since he spoke with a pronounced Oxford accent, I supposed him to be one of the Englishman they had mentioned.

"Oh, yes, I am always English in Ireland," he agreed. "Now in England I am generally French or American but rarely Irish. The English don't think enough of them to hate them—they merely despise them."

As these words lightly tripped from his tongue, I stared at him in alarm. Obviously, he shared Meg's knack for reading thoughts but I doubted he was a banshee. From my limited knowledge of the sect, they were generally women. I did not know about pookas but I rather thought they assumed the shape of a horse and he was much too tall to be a leprechaun. However, there was something familiar about him. I had the sensation one has in crowds sometimes when you glimpse a face you know yet cannot quite place. Quite forgetful of my plight, I considered him dispassionately, attempting to fix his thin, fine features, slightly pointed ears, cat-green eyes, and dark straight hair in the narrow circumference of my acquaintances.

He shook a thin finger at me. "Never try, Miss Ayers; you'd not count me among your friends—nor would you care to call me an enemy, but no matter, I shall be of service to you now. I am in the process of settling some of my accounts and opening new ones."

Approaching me, he quickly and nimbly freed me from my bonds. Indeed, the ropes seemed to unknot themselves. I was glad he had little reason to touch me, for his hands were as cold as frozen iron yet hotter than boiling lead. The closer he came to me, the more my fear and repugnance increased, yet I knew he would do me no bodily harm and that he had no designs upon my soul. That instinctive knowledge was both a relief and a burden, for it served to convince me of my own unimportance in the universe.

He raised his thin brows. "You are wise, Miss Ayers, to guess that you are my instrument and not my victim—it is not the nail that pierces the wood, it is the hammer that drives it home—but the nail has its uses, too. And you are quite right to be afraid—fear is a safeguard against illusion, but no need to be talking to a tongueless woman." He flipped the gag from my mouth and I saw it blacken like a scrap of burning paper in his palm.

He let a rain of ashes drop between his fingers. Then he raised his other hand and behind him the door blew open. Over his shoulder, I saw that dusk had come and the forest was silvered with a fall of moonlight. I longed to be out of the hut and away from his awesome presence, but still I feared those dark confusing woods.

"Go," he advised, "and you'll find your way to those who need you. And if you're asked—you might say, if you've a mind to, that it was Himself who set you free."

"Himself?" I whispered.

"Some call me the rule-maker and others—the rule-breaker."

As I stared at him, I heard a whimpering and a panting and I shrank back as a little furry shape hurtled into the room. It leaped against the leg of the man in green, holding up questing little paws. In the darkness, its eyes flamed like two tiny candles and Himself lifted the creature in his arms and let it lick his face with its long pink tongue, as he murmured soothingly to it. It could have been a dog or a young fox or—

"Brian!" I gasped.

It turned its snout in my direction and snarled.

"No, no, no," murmured Himself. "You're to let her alone—that's the plan." Over the head of the beast, he said, "Miss Ayers, go!"

Without a backward look I ran outside and the sweet air banished the sulfurous odors that had assaulted my nostrils. A small breeze was stirring—it felt like phantom fingers stroking my hair. All about me were the rustlings of the forest, but I, wrapped in the cloak of my strange encounter, was unafraid. I had no idea of where I was going but I knew I had a destination. I continued walking and all of a sudden I heard voices coming from a thicket ahead of me.

"It's perishin' dark, 'ere, Johnny," complained one.

"It'd be better if it was bright sunlight, I suppose, but then there'd be small chance of catchin' the bastards at their dirty work!"

"You suppose we've been told right . . . it's hard to believe the O'Hagans'd be workin' with a band of peasants—an' them rich as kings."

"You can't trust the Irish—high or low an if the information laid against 'em's true, they're in it up to their bloody necks an' they'll hang by 'em, too."

"We've got to find that bridge."

My heart began to pound heavily in my breast. I had to warn Dimitri. Devoutly I prayed to providence or the Devil to guide my steps and soon I was stealing softly away from my countrymen. In another few minutes, I had stepped into a clearing and found the moonlight to be shining on a broad, flowing river. Hastily, I approached, hoping that I would be able to see the outline of the bridge. A second later, a heavy hand fell on my shoulder and I was dragged into the shadows.

120

"By all that's holy, how did you get free?" Lord Concullen's voice whispered in my ear.

I could have told him that "all that's holy" had little to do with my escaping but instead I blurted out, "There are English soldiers in the woods. I heard them talking."

"What?" Dimitri had joined us.

"She's lyin'!" growled Rory.

"Yes, don't believe a word of it," Conan said.

"Please, hear me," I begged. "They say information's been laid against you—and if—if they find you—"

"Hsssst," Tom gasped, for across the clearing several shapes had emerged.

"She's brought 'em with her!" hissed Rory.

Before I could deny it, one of the soldiers groaned, "How'n hell are we goin' to find them—and with them knowing every stick of these woods!?"

"It was said they'd be on this side of the bridge."

"Louder, Roger," snarled another man, "and they'll find us!"

At that, the bushes behind me trembled and out flew the enormous bat I had seen the night of David Fallon's death.

Straight at the soldiers it zoomed, its gigantic wings flapping and the moonlight gleaming on its sharp white fangs. There was a shriek of horror and dismay as it bore one of the men to the ground and sank its teeth into his throat. Two soldiers fired at it but it did not relax its hold, and, with wild screams, the others fled into the darkness.

In another second, the bat had disappeared and in its place stood Uncle Fingal. He wiped a hand across his mouth. "Pah," he spat, "English blood!"

Lord Concullen and Dimitri ran to him and knelt by the fallen man, the rest of us following. As we arrived, Lord Concullen said thankfully, "He's still breathing."

"Look," whispered Tom, "his hair's turned white. Now that's something I never thought I'd see."

"What are we to do with him?" Lord Concullen frowned.

"There's information laid against us," Dimitri said. "Perhaps he'll give us the source of the leak."

"And what about the bridge?" demanded Rory.

"We dare not attempt it tonight," Lord Concullen said decisively. "One of us must get word to the others. Tell them the enemy's been alerted."

No sooner had he finished speaking than I heard the flapping of wings again and saw the bat soar off toward the river. For a moment, I speculated idly on what particular set of rules enabled Uncle Fingal to make these transitions and then all of that was blotted from my mind as Dimitri's arms encircled my waist and his lips met mine.

I could have thought of a hundred objections to his actions—they were not proper, he was an accomplished flirt, he was attached or semi-attached to his cousin Fiona, I was part of his family's plot against the British government, I had known him for less than a fortnight, and what had happened to those former governesses? However, since the salient fact of his lips on mine made protest impossible, I merely slipped my arms around his neck and yielded to the exigencies of the moment.

Except for the time that the butcher boy caught me as I was taking a large order of lamb chops home and was unable to use my hands to defend myself, it was my first kiss. It could certainly rank as the first kiss in which I had so enthusiastically participated, because lamb chops notwithstanding, I had bitten the butcher boy. Though I had had such limited experience, I found that I adapted very well to the situation.

We stole back to the castle by routes which to this day I cannot remember and Dimitri insisted on seeing me to my room. I did not protest because I did not know where Brian might be wandering and though he or it had been docile enough with Himself, I did not want to take any unnecessary chances. Before he left me, Dimitri stood looking down at me for a long time.

"I had not wanted to love you, Lucy," he said at last.

"Because I am a governess?" I asked.

"No—because—whenever I have displayed any partiality for a woman—she—has left me. You will not leave me, will you?" His arms strained around me.

"No, never," I told him fervently.

"Promise!"

I did not scruple to reply, "On my soul."

Dimitri then repeated the action he had initiated in the woods with a few interesting variations. When he finally released me, I gasped, "Oh, I did not know kissing was like that!"

"Does it displease you?"

"On the contrary."

With my tacit consent, he took me in his arms again and as he pressed his lips on mine, he murmured, "Oh, Lucy, Lucy, my beautiful Lucy!"

It was the first time I did not regret my name.

After Dimitri had gone, I slipped into my room, locking my door carefully and undressing quickly. As I was brushing my hair, it occurred to me that possibly my people would dub me traitor. Certainly, I had not furthered Britain's cause in Ireland, but in my own defense I must say that I believe any country big or small has a right to its own way of government, no matter how ill-managed it may appear to outsiders. Having so effectively dispelled any qualms, I went to bed and, somewhat to my surprise, slept very well—waking only when Agnes brought me my morning tea.

# Part Three

WHEN I CAME DOWNSTAIRS THAT MORNING, the O'Hagans greeted me like a heroine—they would not let me attend to my pupils but they would talk to me about my adventures in the forest. Yet I found that I could not tell them about Himself, as often as the true explanation trembled on my lips. Instead, I invented a tale about a kindly stranger, who had discovered and released me, and then I asked some pointed questions of my own.

Lady Kathleen blushed when she admitted that she had indeed hired me at the behest of her husband and his cousins—not for my superior English education but rather for my nationality—as one would throw a handful of sand in their damned eyes. She spoke with a patriotic venom, for which I readily forgave her, while she confessed that on her part, she had long ago forgiven me for being English.

The Princess, too, was less austere and if she were too proud to welcome a governess into her immediate circle, she gave no sign of it. "You have saved my son's life, Miss Ayers," she told me graciously. "For that I must love you."

Lord Concullen was as enthusiastic as he had been on the previous night, but Conan stood apart and, beyond a few murmured congratulations, he said little—only letting his eyes rest on me. I tried to tell myself that, assured of

Dimitri's love as I now was, his cousin no longer had the power to disturb me, but I was forced to admit that I still felt very uneasy in his presence and more than ever wished that he did not reside in the castle. I had similar feelings about their Uncle Fingal and, rather timidly, I inquired if he were about that morning.

"He never emerges from his tomb until after four in the afternoon," Lady Kathleen told me.

"Oh," I said. "I suppose it's that large marble one in the middle of your graveyard?"

"That's right," Lord Concullen answered. "Fingal likes his comfort. Dimitri, I think you should tell Lucy all about him. It would help her to understand him."

"Please do," I said.

"Not at breakfast," begged the Princess.


"Fingal," began Dimitri, some twenty minutes later as we strolled in the garden, "was born in the year 1647 and grew up hearing all the terror tales about Oliver Cromwell's cruelty to the Irish. He was intensely patriotic and he was also very studious—he spent hours in the great library and somehow, we are not sure where he found them, he started reading books on magic—how to summon demons and the like. Well, he shut himself up in a tower room and following the instructions in one of the books, he succeeded in raising a demon. In his diary he——"

"Oh," I interjected, "he kept a diary, too."

Dimitri nodded. "That's how we know most of his story. Do you want me to continue?"

"Oh, yes," I answered quickly, seeing a flicker of impatience in his eyes. Men, I have learned, do not relish having their trains of thoughts derailed. "In his diary . . ." I prompted, helpfully.

"He described the conversation he had had with the demon. It seems that he begged it to help him free Ireland from the English. It promised to consider the matter."

"And did it?" I demanded, adding hastily, "Oh, I'm sorry, please go on."

"Not at the moment. It disappeared. Actually, Fingal should not have consorted with a demon at all, for when you do, you pay a certain price."

"Oh, dear!" I exclaimed, remembering Himself.

"What's the matter now?"

"N-Nothing," I assured him, recalling that I had not, after all, summoned Himself. "What price did Fingal pay? Is that why he is a vampire?"

"It's part of the reason. You see the demon appeared to him again and said it would help him rid the country of the English if he would give it—the heart of his brother's little boy, Niall!"

"Ugh! What a peculiar request."

"I think it's symbolic or something," Dimitri mused. "Anyhow, Fingal was very fond of his nephew and did not want to do it—but he also loved Ireland—and so one night, he put the nurse to sleep with magic spells and took Niall up to his tower room . . . it was there they found him, hours later—the servants, I mean. Niall was asleep on a black-draped altar and lying on the floor was Fingal, a jeweled dagger protruding from his heart."

"My goodness," I exclaimed, "you don't mean that the little boy stabbed him!"

"No, Lucy," Dimitri sighed for some reason. "After he had risen from his grave, Fingal explained to his brother that he had meant to kill Niall but that when he had lifted up his dagger to perform the deed, the child had reached for it, laughing and cooing as if it were some pretty toy. He could not bear to harm him and, in horror and shame, he drove the weapon into his own heart—and the demon, finding him dying, had angrily condemned him to be a vampire."

"Oh," I said, "it's a very sad story, but don't vampires have to—to—?"

"They do," Dimitri nodded, "but the peasants around here are fiercely loyal and they believed that even if he did consort with demons, he died a hero's death—they actually prefer demons to the English, I think, and so generations of them have voluntarily supplied him with—uh—sustenance. He never takes enough to hurt them—he wouldn't dream of harming an Irishman."

"I gather he has fewer compunctions about the British," I gulped.

"As a member of the O'Hagan clan, you will be safe," Dimitri kissed me.

"Oh, that's nice," I told him, dismissing Uncle Fingal from my mind and replacing him with Fiona, yet another disturbing element. I had not seen her at breakfast and had thus been spared the sight of her distress and possible anger. Yet, I had considerable qualms about our next meeting, for I wondered how I could concoct an explanation of the events leading to my conquest of the man whom she had told me was promised to her. In spite of my very real love for Dimitri, I could find it in my heart to pity poor Fiona, bereft as she was of David Fallon and with no chance of regaining her cousin's affections—that is, if she ever really had them. I admit that I may seem a trifle spiteful, but I must excuse myself by saying that I believed Fiona's passion for Dimitri to be of a rather intermittent nature—judging by the tender scene I had witnessed from my window.

Pondering on David Fallon's untimely death, I wondered, too, what had made Fiona so sure that her brother had killed him. I found myself agreeing with Dimitri that Brian, little as he was, could scarcely have attacked a grown man. Yet, if it were not Brian, who—or what—had murdered David? I wanted to accept the ready explanation of a wild beast but found myself strangely uneasy about it. As far as I knew, the only wild beasts that dwelt in Irish forests were the smaller variety of rodent, foxes and deer—animals with neither the inclination nor the means to tear out a man's throat. On the other hand there had been my unsettling experience with that nameless, glaring presence in the bushes. However, if I could not be satisfied as to the manner in which David Fallon had met his end, I was glad that I could at least give poor Fiona some small comfort—at least she need no longer bear the burden of her brother's guilt.

"Lucy, you are still looking very grave." Dimitri pulled me toward him and stared down into my eyes.

"I—was thinking about Fiona," I told him frankly. "I really ought to find her and explain . . ."

"Explain what?" he asked.

Surprised at his obtuseness, I said, "She told me there was an attachment between you—one of long standing."

"Why—yes, there is an attachment—we are cousins." A gleam of amusement appeared in his eyes. "Or did she lead you to believe it was something more serious?"

It was not a time to honor confidences. "Well, yes, she did."

He laughed. "Poor little Fiona, such a romantic child."

"There—is an understanding, then?"

130

"I understand—*her,*" he laughed, then grew grave. "I am afraid that poor Fiona had formed a far more lasting attachment for David."

"Poor Fiona," I sighed.

He shrugged. "Ah, well, she will have a dozen more lovers before she's seventeen. Kathie has it in mind to send her to Paris."

Feeling considerably cheered by this information, I continued walking with him. He really did not have much to say to me as we promenaded among the trees, but I found his silences far more effective than words, even though I felt that I should, in the interests of decorum and the two under-gardeners, repulse his ardor. I said as much but he only laughed and, my impulses being more honest than my training, I ceased to protest. Yet, even though I enjoyed our promenade, I could not put from my mind the small nagging fact of Fiona. When we parted, I hoped that I would find her somewhere downstairs—I rather shrank from going to her room without invitation. As it happens, I encountered her in the great hall.

She was still in her mourning black but it occurred to me that she looked much more cheerful than she had on the previous day. As I tried to think what I would say to her, she danced up to me and seized my hands. "Lucy, my darling bosom friend and cousin-to-be!" she exclaimed.

If she had flung a firebrand in my face I could not have been more astonished. "You—heard and—"

"Certainly. Kathie told me. Oh, I am so proud of you. I never heard of anything so brave—betraying your own countrymen to save Dimitri!"

Though I could not like the way she put it, she seemed quite unconscious of having made any slur against my character and her blue eyes shone innocently into mine. She looked, in fact, as I remembered her that first day when I had thought her the most beautiful and gracious little girl I had ever seen.

"But I thought you told me that you and Dimitri . . ."

"Oh, I was making it up, Lucy. I was instructed to do so by Aunt Kathie—it was all part of the master plan."

"Master plan?"

"You know why they hired you, don't you?" she asked with an anxious little frown.

"Yes, they told me."

"Oh, good," she clapped her hands. "Well, when you arrived they were thunderstruck because they had never expected an Englishwoman to be so beautiful—so they told me that it was my duty to keep you from trying to charm Dimitri—he is very susceptible, you know, and it certainly would have complicated matters if he had fallen in love with an Englishwoman. You, however, are different. Why, Aunt Kathie thinks you are almost Irish and, believe me, that is a very great compliment."

I tried to look duly flattered. "Then—all you told me about those other governesses—that wasn't the truth?"

"Oh, yes, it was true—but that shouldn't worry you, Lucy. They just got bored and went off—it happens all the time, as you would have found out if you had continued in your profession. And I, for one, am certainly glad that they did—because it gave us the opportunity to hire you and I do love you, Lucy." She embraced me rapturously. "And have you heard? Aunt Kathie is sending me to Paris. Lucy, even if you are going to marry Dimitri and be a lady of the manor, will you continue to help me with my French verbs?"

Though I was somewhat taken aback by her high spirits so soon after her cousin's death, it was with considerable relief that I embraced her and said, "Of course, I shall be delighted." And then, I told her the good news about Brian.


My diary, as you can imagine, was very full; I had written far more than its dated pages allowed. The description of that one night ran from September 24 through December 16th but though only seventeen pages remained for my eager pen, I felt secure in writing finis to my adventures at O'Hagan's Keep. I really did not see how any more could happen to me. I had decided to stop comparing my life with that of Jane Eyre, for really, it was a silly conceit in the first place—every heroine must find her own destiny. Yet, as I sat over my diary that night, I must say that I preened myself a little—I had certainly achieved happiness and the master or at least one of the masters of the castle in considerably less time than it had taken Jane Eyre. I went to bed with ink on my fingers and glory in my heart.

I awoke the next morning with the cry of the banshee in my ears and, running to the window, I saw Meg, standing on her rock, her face as pale as sea foam, wailing her awful warning to the turbulent wind-tossed waves.

"Meg," I shrieked. "Who!"

She ignored my questions and continued her plaint. I dressed hastily and rushed downstairs to the breakfast room. The O'Hagans were all assembled and I could see from their grave looks that I did not have to tell them of the warning I had heard.

"What can it mean?" I cried.

It was Lady Kathleen who alerted me to at least one imminent danger. "Patrick and Dimitri are going—hunting this morning."

"Hunting?" I cried. "For what?"

Dimitri took my hands. "For what we must find . . ." he said.

"But—you've been warned. You heard . . ."

"We're in no peril," Lord Concullen soothed me, "it's only a meeting."

"But—if—if there's a traitor—how can you be sure you'll not be discovered and—and—"

"Lucy," Lady Kathleen said, "it does no good to argue with them. That's something you must learn about O'Hagan men."

I stared at their implacable faces and burst into tears, but though Dimitri comforted me, he also left me—and I, watching him ride away with Lord Concullen, wondered if I would ever see him again. As I turned back to the house, I thought drearily that I would have to amend my diary.

To occupy my time, I insisted on teaching and bore my young charges off to the schoolroom. Brian had not yet rejoined us and I must say that I was glad. In spite of my very deep sympathy for the child, I did not think I could face him with equanimity just yet—especially after our encounter in the hut. Nor did I understand how he had escaped a second time. Danny, who had been looking after him, insisted that something had come through the window and knocked him out, but as the window had been shut fast, Lady Kathleen was inclined to believe that Danny's enemy had been the bottle of Irish whiskey found emptied beneath his chair. It did occur to me that Uncle Fingal might have had a hand or claw in it, but as I was soon to be his in-law, I tried to ignore my suspicions. It is bad enough being related by marriage to a vampire without suspecting him of having designs on your life—though Dimitri had quelled some of my fears in that regard. I cannot say that knowing his history made me like him any better, but I did pity him and I believed that in time I could even face him without shuddering. Oddly enough, I had less tolerance for Brian, even though I have always abhorred bats and thought nothing in particular about wolves. Werewolves, however, are another matter and faced with the O'Hagan penchant for protecting their afflicted, living and dead, I could only hope that an aspiring doctor might be able to find a treatment for lycanthropy, or better yet that Brian might outgrow his tendencies.

After lunch, I took my pupils for a walk in the gardens and then I resumed lessons but, as the afternoon wore on, my attention often wandered. I could not rid myself of the feeling of impending doom nor could I forget the banshee's cry. In my mind's eye, I pictured Dimitri dead or dying. Finally, I could bear the confinement of the schoolroom no longer. Dismissing Kevin and Marra, I went back into the gardens. It was getting on toward five o'clock and a scattering of clouds was passing over the sun, dappling the trees and grass with a patchwork of light. A wind had arisen and rustled among the trees, loosening some of the dead leaves. I usually like autumn but then, for the first time, I experienced its reputed melancholy and unwillingly my eyes went from the blooming dahlias to the drooping roses. Even the butterflies that still fluttered above the hardier blossoms seemed ready to end their short lives, leaving their bodies to the scavenger ants. Sighing, I made my way across the fading grass to a stone bench that stood near a little fountain. Sinking down, I watched the play of the water issuing from the conch shell a marble mermaid had lifted to her pretty lips. It was a charming statue, but I saw that a coating of moss bearded her plump cheeks and that a dead bird floated in the pool of water below her. Wearily, I leaned my head back against a tree that stood behind the bench and closed my eyes. Perhaps I dozed a little, for Fiona's voice, when I heard it, seemed to come from the other end of a long dark tunnel.

"Lucy, Lucy, wake up—for God's sake, Lucy!"

I opened my eyes, blinking up at Fiona, who stood over

me, agitated and tearful. "You're crying," I said stupidly. "Why are you crying, Fiona?"

"Lucy, I've been looking for you everywhere! It's D-Dimitri. Oh, I don't know how to tell you this—I really don't." Great sobs welled up from her throat, her eyes brimmed and overflowed.

"Dimitri? What happened—is—is he?"

"He's hurt badly, Lucy. Oh, why did you hide yourself in these gardens? I thought I'd never find you and—and now it may be too late. Oh, please—you must come with me. Hurry!"

I got to my feet, hoping against hope that I was still dreaming, but I knew that I was wide awake. "What happened to him?"

"He—he was shot by the—the soldiers," Fiona sobbed. "Oh, Lucy, come—we must go to him. Thank God, the tide's not in, yet."

"The—tide?"

"Patrick had him carried to the sea caves—we dared not hide him in the castle. They'd come looking for him."

"The sea caves?"

"Yes, beneath the cliffs—they are a hiding place for the Brotherhood—but come, I'll tell you the rest later . . . There's no more time to be lost—I—I promised him I'd bring you before—"

"Is he—beyond help?" I asked numbly.

She nodded. "Kathleen has sent for the doctor—but he has lost so much blood."

Hardly aware of what I was doing, I let her lead me through the garden to a small door I had never noticed before. In another second, I found myself outside the walls and soon we had reached the cliffs. Fiona showed me where to climb over the small parapet and as we came down on the other side, she ran quickly to a thorny mass of bushes and thick green plants. Indicating it, she said, "There's an entrance to the grottoes through here—no one knows about it—except a few of us." Pulling the bushes aside, she pointed and I looked down into a forbidding dark hole.

"How—can anyone get down there?" I faltered.

"It is possible. I have done it—and so has Patrick. It's the fastest way—if—if we are to reach him before———" She bit her lip and said stoically, "There's no time for tears now. Are you ready, Lucy? Patrick gave me candles to light our way." She fumbled in her pocket and brought up a stubby white piece of wax and a flint.

"Yes, I'll go," I said. At that moment, I would have entered the mouth of hell—for Dimitri.

I shall never forget that descent into the bowels of the earth—the narrow way of sliding rocks and slippery dirt, the treacherous toeholds, the rocky walls slimy under my hands and growing colder and wetter as we descended. I was sure that I would never reach the bottom alive but finally the rocks ceased to slide—finally, I stood with Fiona on wet, close-packed sand and somewhere in the distance, I heard the pounding of the sea. Fiona held up her candle—the tiny flame illumined a stalactite-hung interior.

"Come," she whispered as before, and we made our way through a labyrinth of rocks.

"Where is he?" I cried, and my voice echoed hollowly in that vast interior . . . "He, he, he, he."

"We shall be with him soon," she called back, and the walls boomed "Soon, soon, soon."

Yet we could not hurry and our progress was rendered the more difficult because my skirt so often caught on the crystallized protuberances arising from the floor and from the walls as well. Occasionally, the passage between them was so narrow that we had to edge along sideways and at other times we had to crouch down to avoid hitting our heads on the roof of the cavern, but at last I saw light ahead—light that illumined the crystalline deposits in the caves so that they shone with an eerie beauty I could not appreciate.

"We are coming to the central caverns, Lucy," Fiona said. "We are almost there." She hurried to my side and, seizing my hand, pulled me forward toward the light which increased in intensity as we neared it. "Come, Lucy, come, come, come!"

She moved too quickly for me—half stumbling, I rushed after her through a huge natural archway into a great shining room, so bright indeed that I blinked and for the moment could see nothing except whirls of dancing patterns before my eyes, and, on Fiona's releasing her hold, I lost my balance and fell prone on the floor.

"Oh, Lucy," she gasped, "did I hurt you?"

I shook my head, and into my nostrils seeped the most

peculiar odor—a heavy, sweet scent completely obliterating the smell of seaweed. I sniffed at it, surprised. "What's that?" I asked her. "It can't be perfume!"

"Ambergris, my dear," remarked a man's voice.

Rising, I saw a tall figure in the brown habit of a monk. A hood shadowed his face, and, to me, he looked the very picture of doom. "Father," I cried, "is—Dimitri still alive?"

The monk raised his hands in a gesture of benediction. "Child," he whispered, "I think so."

"Oh, take me to him—quickly!" I begged.

"My dear child," he said gently, "calm yourself." Reaching out a slender hand, he patted my cheek.

I stiffened—for I knew the touch; I knew the voice, too. "Conan!" I cried incredulously.

"The same," he said, lifting his hood.

A terrible fear overtook me. "But—where's Dimitri?"

"That need not concern you, Lucy." Fiona faced me, her eyes blazing with an evil light. "As I once told you, Dimitri is mine!"

Conan laughed. "My niece is a formidable rival, Miss Ayers—as well as a gifted actress, as I am sure you will agree—having been treated to her histrionics."

"Actress!" I gasped. "It was a trick—all a trick!"

"You have your tricks and I, mine, Lucy," she agreed complacently. "I think we need not dispute as to which are the more effective."

Even in what I recognized as my deadly peril, I could say thankfully, "Dimitri is safe, then?"

"Safely pursuing traitors," sneered Conan, "for he's still young enough to believe in the Cause, and stupid enough to imagine the Irish yearn for freedom."

"That is not what I call stupidity," I cried.

"Is it not? What would they do with freedom, pray?" Conan asked me. "It's the lack of it that saves them. All Irishmen were born to fight—if it were not the English, it would be each other, and they'd be one with the dinosaur and the dodo—so I say, Long live the English on our Irish soil!"

"It was you," I accused, "you who informed on your own clan!"

He shrugged. "Like you, my dear, I am not overtroubled with patriotic fervor. Yes, I informed on them—I am

selfish enough to want this castle for my own uses . . .
These grottoes are sadly inaccessible . . ."

"You—put Dimitri in danger!" Fiona hissed suddenly.
"You'll regret that. I'll tell . . ."

He whirled away from me and, looking down on her
answered softly, "Tell what . . . have you ever thought
what I might tell about you, if I chose, dear Fiona?"

As they confronted each other, I made a desperate
effort to flee that cavern, but even as I started to run,
Conan, moving with lightning speed, caught me and pin-
ioned my arms behind my back, while Fiona, hurrying
after us, dealt me a stinging slap across the mouth. She
had raised her hand to repeat the cruel blow when Conan
said sharply:

"Enough! After I am done with her, it will be your
turn." He smiled at me. "You must not be afraid of *me. I*
shall not harm you. You are about to participate in a very
edifying, not to say educational, ceremony—one that few
have had the opportunity of witnessing in this prudish and
hypocritical age. You will make a most delightful acolyte,
for you are far better endowed than either of the two
other young women my niece brought me."

"The other governesses," I cried. "Oh, God!"

"It's Satan you must call on here—or Himself, if you
prefer," Conan told me.

"Uncle Conan, it's getting late and soon the moon will
rise," Fiona said softly, her eyes gleaming oddly. Staring
at them, I had a sudden memory of my initial terror in
the woods.

"Your eyes!" I gasped, and then fell silent as I saw
Conan's horrified expression. He had actually turned pale.

"You—do right to—to remind me, my own. We—must
not be t-together when the—s-sun sets," he stammered.
"I—I'd not relish the fate of David Fallon."

"Be silent!" she commanded fiercely.

"The fate of David Fallon?" I exclaimed.

"When the madness comes over my niece, she is not in
the least selective," Conan said. "Like her mother before
her, she kills any human being she encounters. One wonders what will happen to Dimitri."

"Nothing!" cried Fiona. "Nothing, I tell you."

"A nothing such as the nothing that destroyed his
father and yours?" inquired Conan sweetly. "But we must

138

not dwell on such painful topics—not when we have such rare pleasures before us."

He dragged me into a smaller cavern, and before me I saw a long narrow table draped with a black velvet cloth stitched with strange scarlet symbols. Over it was suspended a cross which appeared to be upside down. Golden candelabra, grotesquely carved, threw their light on tapestried walls. Staring at them, I exclaimed in horrified amazement, for certainly their subject matter was most unusual!

"Fiona," Conan said, "help me."

"Yes, Uncle." She picked up something from the table and turned back, a knife in her hand. I saw it flash toward me and heard a rending sound. My garments gaped open and she pulled them roughly from me until I stood shivering and naked. Then Conan lifted me high in his arms and bore me to that table. I screamed—and as the sound tore from my throat, I heard an answering cry,

"Lucy, Lucy, where are you!" It was Dimitri's voice.

"Dimitri!" Fiona screamed, unbelieving, and, suddenly, he was there in the chamber, and with him was Uncle Fingal, his eyes blazing red and his pale lips drawn back to expose two gleaming fangs.

Conan released me quickly. "What are you . . . ?"

"Traitor!" screamed Uncle Fingal, "I know all . . . the English dogs confessed. On your knees ere I——"

"Dimitri," Fiona cried, "look at Lucy—she is a witch— a witch. I found her out—she and Uncle Conan together planned your—betrayal, and it—it was she who murdered David Fallon!"

Before I could refute this terrible accusation, Uncle Fingal had rushed across the room, his hands, talon-like, ready to seize Conan's throat.

"Keep away from me, Fingal!" Conan thundered. "We serve the same master!"

In that moment, Uncle Fingal came to a halt, an expression of dismay on his saturnine features. "We do, but . . ."

"But—you cannot touch me!" Conan told him triumphantly.

"We'll see about that," returned Uncle Fingal, reaching for him. Then he groaned, for his hands seemed to encounter an invisible wall. He beat against this barrier futilely, and, at last, he groaned again. "It's no use . . .

no use . . . he speaks the truth, damn him. Oh, I am accursed—accursed."

"You have known that for two centuries," Conan retorted, "so how dared you bring Dimitri here!"

"No matter," Dimitri said, striding to my side. "I am here and in time to save my darling." Tearing the cloak he wore from his shoulders, he draped it about me. Seizing one of the candelabra, he said, "Come, my love. Come with me!"

Fiona rushed to us. "Dimitri, did you not hear what I said—she . . . she . . ." Suddenly, her voice broke and changed into a snarling cry, and she fell to the floor, her body quivering all over as if seized with a sudden ague.

"The sun . . . the sun has set!" screamed Conan.

"Come, Lucy, come quickly," Dimitri cried, dragging me away—but not before I had seen Fiona's face lengthen and turn into a larger replica of Brian's visage, as I had seen it that night with Himself. Behind us, as we dashed through the aperture into the greater cavern, there was a long wolf howl, a ferocious snarl, and then a gurgling scream.

Dimitri, hastening his steps, pushed me into the narrow tunnel through which I had come before. We stumbled along frantically, until, suddenly, he stopped and groaned.

"What is it?" I cried.

"Look!" he said despairingly.

Confronting us was a network of small passageways. "Which one do we take?" I demanded.

"I don't know," he answered. "Fingal and I entered the grottoes from the sea. Lucy, we—we're lost."

"Oh, my love," I whispered, "I don't care—as long as we're together."

In that moment, darkness fell and a chill grasp met mine. "Come," a familiar voice whispered in my ear. "Come—both of you," it said.

Dazed, I felt myself propelled, with Dimitri, through the Stygian blackness. The hand that held mine was colder than winter seawater, but I was no longer frightened as back we went through the labyrinthian caves, up the sliding path, through a curtain of vines to the welcome air. As we stood there, Dimitri and I, locked in each other's arms, waves higher than I had ever seen them plunged into the sea grottoes. For the first time in my life, I fainted.

Not surprisingly, my unaccustomed exposure to the elements resulted in a severe chill and it was three days before I felt well enough to sit up. It was then that Dimitri told me how two fishermen had found the savaged corpse of Conan O'Hagan, lying on the rocks outside the flooded caves. But what had horrified them even more had been the carcass of a young shewolf, which, as they had touched it, had turned back into the limp, drowned body of Fiona O'Hagan.

As for our rescue, I must be grateful to Meg, the banshee, even though I cannot help resenting her reasons for it, which I learned on the morning I was to wed Dimitri O'Hagan.

"It's leavin' you I'll be this day," she called to me from her perch beside the sea.

"What?" I cried. "The Curse of the Concullens has come to pass?"

"It will soon."

I am sure the color drained from my cheeks. I clutched my heart. "What—what will it be?" I asked fearfully. "Can you tell me?"

"That I can. Look in your mirror an' you'll find it starin' back at you!"

"Why—why—what do you mean?" I demanded.

"Well, if all those five O'Hagan brothers I used to know nated one thing more than life itself, it was the English that was overrunnin' Irish sod, an' now I've fixed it that there'll be an English bride in the chapel of which they was so proud—it's to be hoped that the roof will not fall in—and sure they must be all spinnin' in their graves, especially Dermot that wronged me . . . though he was a good lover, I'll grant him that . . . but ssssst, what's this?"

She stiffened and stared. Following her gaze, I saw a great black horse loom up on the road before us. Astride him was a handsome young man with a head of bright golden hair and the look of Patrick O'Hagan, except that he wore a scarlet doublet and had a great white ruff to circle his throat. Audaciously, he rode up to Meg and, reaching out a long arm, scooped her into it and lifted her onto his saddle bow.

"Come, fairy maid," I heard him whisper in a voice like the wind through the trees. "We're off to the green forests!"

I saw her hands beating against his breast, but before

she could open her mouth to protest, he had pressed a long kiss on her lips and then, turning his mettlesome mount, he galloped off with her into a sun that gleamed through both of them.

If Meg's revenge on the O'Hagans was not quite as complete as she had planned, I cannot believe it was repugnant to her—for before they faded from view, I saw her fling her arms around him and pillow her fiery head on his shoulder.


Fortunately, for my peace of mind, the O'Hagans did not seem to be aware of their doom—they welcomed me with as much enthusiasm as if I had been born Irish. However, since I was not entirely a Hibernian, I had a heart-to-heart talk with Dimitri.

"You are not to go out fighting the English, again," I told him sternly. "Death and destruction are never a solution to any problem. I have a much better way to deal with them."

"What's that?" he demanded.

"You must stand for Parliament," I said. "An Irishman can win any argument!"

"But—my accent," he protested.

"My love, I am not an English teacher for nothing," I responded complacently. "In time you will speak as brilliantly as any Demosthenes."

"With a Greek accent? That wouldn't help me either," he laughed, and then he kissed me. "My amazing Lucy, you are quite right—and besides I dearly love to talk."

"I guessed as much," I told him demurely.


We were married at high noon and I was told that I made a very beautiful bride in my heavy white satin, billowing over the largest crinoline I could find, my trailing lace veil, and my perfectly matched pearls. It was a lovely ceremony; both our families were there and everybody cried happily, even little Brian, who, dressed in a blue velvet suit as my ring-bearer, looked so cherubic that I, with a thrill of new family pride, kissed him almost without a tremor. Indeed, I was so ecstatic over my "happy ending," as it were, that I knew I would be able to put up with all the other horrors in the castle and, who knows, I might even grow to be on good terms with the irascible Fitz. And as I have mentioned, I had every reason to be in accord with Uncle Fingal, now completely recovered from his ordeal in the cave. I do think you ought to be tolerant about spirits for, without being too morbid about it, you never know what destiny has in store for you, once you are freed from what Shakespeare so aptly termed "mortal coils."

The aftermath of the ceremony proved to be exhausting and full of confusion, which I must say was augmented by Mama, who tearfully told me, "My darling Oriana, about the—the cabbage leaves, I meant to . . ." Before she could conclude her sentence, one of my younger brothers fell into the fountain and I never did hear what she had intended to say.

It was with considerable relief that I finally parted from the assembled guests and retired with my husband to the chamber he said we would both be sharing now.

It was very large and its chief article of furniture was an immense bed brought from Italy by an O'Hagan ancestor. It rested on swans' wings and had a canopy of dark blue velvet stitched on the inside with little glittering stars. Since it was the only bed in the room, I shared that with Dimitri, too—and a few instructive hours later, I suddenly said to him, "Dimitri, is *this* the fate worse than death?"

He laughed loudly. "It has been called that . . . but . . . we're married now, so it doesn't matter."

"Oh," I sighed rapturously. "Lovely." And lying back against the lacy pillows, I abandoned myself to my fate again.

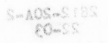

## About the Author

FLORENCE STEVENSON has always had a predilection for good fiction, frank humor, and matters mysterious. She has two successful novels, *Ophelia* and *A Feast of Eggshells*—both on the supernatural side. In 1969 her play *Chronicle* was produced by the Chelsea Theater Center in Brooklyn, New York. Currently, she is writing another fanciful novel, a project she is fitting in between assignments for *Opera News, Weight Watchers Magazine,* and the Metropolitan Opera–Philharmonic Hall programs—publications with which she has long been affiliated. Miss Stevenson comes from Los Angeles but currently lives in New York with a cat named Zodiac, who, she says, looks better in the cover picture than she does.